B at Home

Emma Moves again

By Valérie Besanceney

Summertime Publishing
by your side from inspiration to publication

"Beautifully written with wonderful things that children can relate to, I can see *B at Home: Emma Moves Again* being used in families by parents who care about their upcoming move. Local and international schools will love it because their students deal with transitions and more and more are becoming TCKs. Adults who work with families in global transition will find this wonderful book by Valérie Besanceney added to their 'go to shelf'. Little tidbits such as '... home will never ever be one place. It will be constantly moving. Like the waves, like the beads in the kaleidoscope' has made *B at Home: Emma Moves Again* one of my favorite books.

Many people think fondly of Winnie-the-Pooh, and one of my favorite quotes by A.A. Milne is 'How lucky I am to have something that makes saying goodbye so hard'. Pooh and B have a lot in common. They both support the child that loves them. B, the bear, is a wiser and more experienced voice of reason that helps children as they work through the issues that happen when parents take on a global lifestyle. Besanceney's bear is even more powerful for the expat community."

Julia Simens,
Author, *Emotional Resilience and the Expat Child: practical storytelling techniques that will strengthen the global family*

"This book is a 'must read' for anyone moving with young children. The concepts are very salient within the TCK/ expat culture, including the ambivalence of leaving one place and moving to another, along with being okay with enjoying one's new environment. Valérie Besanceney captures the experience, and the wisdom exhibited through the teddy bear makes it much more poignant. This is a book that will help children and their parents (and stuffed animals!) with any transition or move."

Dr Lisa Pittman,
Co-author, *Expat Teens Talk*

"This is a 'must read' for parents and young children on the move. It addresses emotions related to change and transition in the face of an international relocation. Having experienced eight international moves with our growing family, we have seen, felt and been through the uncertainties, fear, and excitement of impending change. I wish *B at Home: Emma Moves Again* had been available to read to and share with my children when they were younger.

Valérie Besanceney has provided us with an easy to read, informative, supportive, practical 'how to guide' through her enjoyable story as shared with the fun, thoughtful and real characters of B and Emma. She identifies issues and challenges related to change, including language, new culture, and losing one's sense of belonging. She also offers practical strategies to help children take their precious memories of one country and the life they have lived in it, while transitioning to the next. Valérie's book is real, relatable and enjoyable. It would be a great tool for classroom teachers of young children, especially those in international schools with high student population turnovers.

I am already looking forward to the changing adventures of Emma's life and hope Valérie writes the sequel sharing what happens during the teenage years of Emma's transient life."

Diana Smit,
Co-author, *Expat Teens Talk*

First Edition 2014
First Published in the United Kingdom by Summertime Publishing

ISBN 978-1-909193-45-1

Designed by Owen Jones, www.owenjonesdesign.com

Illustrated by Agnes Loonstra, www.agnesloonstra.nl

'Fourteen Angels' adapted from 'Evening Prayer' from the opera
Hansel and Gretel by Engelbert Humperdinck

"Ruth, wherever you go in life, unpack your bags –
physically and mentally – and plant your trees."
– *Charles Frame*

"All you have to be is you."
– *Anonymous*

For
Josephine Scout
and
Madeleine Sage

Acknowledgements

This book would have never been possible without the inspiration, encouragement, and support from Ruth Van Reken, Jo Parfitt, Sheila Schenkel, Jane Dean, Anja Wortman, Mark Nunn, Noreen Jilani, Doug Osbo, Stephen Swecker, and Kathy Palmer. Fiona van Dijk-Janssens, thank you for letting me borrow Emma's name and for proving that some friendships last – no matter how many moves. Mammie and Pappie, thank you from the bottom of my heart for the journey that has allowed me to grow into the person I am. Todd, Josephine and Madeleine – you are my favorite home. B, thank you for always being there.

Contents

Foreword

You are holding an amazing book in your hands. For years I have traveled the globe seeking to help third culture kids (TCKs)[1], adult TCKs, their parents, educators, and all who work with this population to better understand not only the effects of a globally mobile childhood, but also how to help children navigate the challenges well so they can use the rich resources of this experience throughout life. But I will confess one thing. The biggest challenge I face in all these journeys is how to communicate the concepts and strategies for success in an effective way to the TCKs themselves. At international schools I happily hold sessions for adult TCKs, educators, and parents, but gulp big time when told I will be facing the students, particularly the younger ones. I organize panels and interactive activities with the high schoolers, but how to translate these vital concepts so younger children can understand and use them? For me, that is hard.

I admit some people are surprised to hear me say this. After all, isn't my life's work about helping the children? Yes and no.

----

1   TCKs were first identified in the early 1950s by American sociologist and anthropologist Ruth Hill Useem, 'to refer to the children who accompany their parents into another society'. This was further expanded by David C. Pollock and Ruth E. Van Reken: 'A third culture kid is a person who has spent a significant part of his or her developmental years outside their parents' culture. The third culture kid builds relationships to all the cultures, while not having full ownership in any. Although elements from each culture are assimilated into the third culture kid's life experience, the sense of belonging is in relationship to others of the same background, other TCKs'.

In personality and thinking style, I am better suited to educating adults rather than children. My focus is often trying to help parents, or those who work with TCKs, to develop understanding and strategies to help them thrive. In addition, when I first heard the term *third culture kid*, I was in my late thirties. At that point it described the life I had already lived. I felt great relief in knowing there was a concept and language to describe the experience, and my responses to it, which I previously thought were mine alone. But if someone had told me when I was a child, or during my teenage years, that these characteristics common to the TCK experience were who I was because I had grown up between an African and a US American world, I would have said, 'No, I'm not like that and I won't be'. And I'm sure I would have set out to prove that person wrong. No one likes to be put in an arbitrary box – especially children in the process of that wonderful process of self-discovery of learning what it means to be 'me'. They want to know who they are as a unique individual – different from all others in the world, yet needing connection and belonging to those same 'others'. If they don't have some understanding of the larger context of their individual story, even today's TCKs can feel as I did so long ago, 'What's the matter with *me*?' rather than accepting what are normal feelings for those growing up internationally.

But here is the good news – for me and for you. In this delightful book, *B at Home: Emma Moves Again*, you have the solution for how to translate what we as adults know about the TCK experience, into language and concepts that children who grow up globally can relate to.

Children who read this will enjoy the story and perhaps be surprised to find someone else putting words on feelings they have known. Because it *is* a story, the feelings are safe to connect with because they feel familiar, but no one is 'telling them' who they are or what they are 'supposed' to feel. In discussion with parents or educators, B and Emma's feelings can be examined for what they are, while leaving open the possibility for self-discovery during that process. Parents or other adults reading the story can see into the heart of B and Emma and begin to understand how a child's viewpoint and feelings may be quite different from those of the parents when it comes to moving.

But far more than an exercise in 'Tell me how you feel or felt ...' this book offers clear strategies for parents, educators, others who work with TCKs, and the TCKs themselves, on practical ways to translate theory into plans and practices to help children navigate well the chronic cycles of separation inherent in a TCK's childhood. If you look you will find tucked away in this wonderful story the common responses of family members as they go through transition.

In addition, you will identify the principles and practical strategies you can use to help build resiliency in children as they experience each transition. You will discover them as you read along with your child and see how B and Emma – and the adults around them – found ways, in the end, of ultimately making this an enriching experience for them all.

Common responses to transition:
1. Parents and others encouraging the child before comforting (is it one way parents deal with a sense of guilt that they are 'doing this' to their child?)
2. Friends withdrawing when hearing the child will be moving
3. Fear to move to the future for fear of denying the past

Practical strategies to help:
1. Comforting before encouraging
2. Leaving well to ultimately enter a new place well
3. Developing portable traditions
4. Preparing linguistically for the next school if the new instructional language is different from that at home
5. Allowing the child to carry 'sacred objects' to connect their worlds
6. Ensuring a child has at least one language deep enough to think in
7. Allowing the normal process of grief
8. Planning ahead – allowing a child to have a say in making the next place 'theirs'
9. Being intentional in finding ways to enter the new place well
10. Staying in contact with old friends while making new ones

Thank you B, thank you Emma, thank you Valérie, for showing how even the challenges of the TCK experience can be turned into some of our greatest gifts.

Ruth E. Van Reken
Co-author, *Third Culture Kids: Growing Up Among Worlds*
Co-founder, Families in Global Transition, www.FIGT.org

Introduction

Ever since we moved away from my house – my home – in the Netherlands for the first time, when I was five years old, I have struggled with the definition of 'home'. As a child I remember thinking, *I just want to go home*, not knowing what or where that was anymore. Growing into a typical chameleon TCK (third culture kid), I identified with my Dutch cousins, my international school friends, and the local neighborhood children, wherever 'local' happened to be.

As a teenager I had heard the term 'global nomads', but somehow believed that losing my sense of roots and belonging was a 'trivial problem' of a child lucky enough to have the incredibly enriching experiences of traveling around. Having the opportunity to see more of the world, I couldn't justify making a fuss out of moving.

My most profound connections were often with peers from countries I had never been to, but who had a similar upbringing. We had the common ground of never being in one place for very long. We would immediately recognize those familiar words of, 'It's complicated' to the question, 'Where are you from?' However, the sense of not truly feeling at home anywhere, yet being able to blend in everywhere, began to tug at the seams of my soul.

By the time I was in my mid-twenties, I had tried my luck looking for home in the USA, Germany, France, Switzerland and the Netherlands. The country I mostly identified with was the Netherlands, but when I was there I felt like a fish out of water. Being anywhere for a long time made me restless and the constant moving had become a home of sorts. The one place I started to think of as home was a little town in the Swiss Alps where I had built memories every year from the age of four.

By officially accepting my favorite little Swiss town, Gryon, as 'home', an actual physical place I could be in, leave, and come back to, I realized there was still a whole big world out there to discover. It was in Gryon that I fell in love with the man who would eventually become my husband. We share a passion for teaching and traveling and decided to combine the two by working in international schools. I temporarily stopped pining for home, we packed our bags and we traveled and moved around. A lot.

It was only when we began talking about starting our own family that my pull for Switzerland, for going home, became stronger. I wanted to be closer to my parents, my family, closer to my one place that felt like home. I knew I wanted our future children to have some roots, especially if we were to move somewhere else with them one day.

When I began my career as a teacher I read *Third Culture Kids: Growing Up Among Worlds* by David C. Pollock and Ruth E. Van Reken. I immediately felt an overwhelming sense of recognition and relief. It finally all made sense. They described my experience better than I'd ever been able to myself. It quickly became one of my most coveted books. Not only were my feelings about growing up a TCK clarified, they were also validated. The emotions connected to my search for home were acceptable and normal, and not a trivial problem to suppress. What I needed to figure out was how to come to terms with the challenges of my global life and truly benefit from this amazing journey.

Adult TCKs often talk about the challenges of their constant moving as children, and can only reflect on the positive influences of their nomadic existence later in life. I know I silently struggled as a child, and there were only a handful of educators along the way who showed empathy for my situation. As a teacher, I have

Introduction

become passionate about the 'third culture kid phenomenon'. In the classroom, I try to ensure that my students who are, or who will be, relocated get a chance to reflect on their situation, to say their 'goodbyes' and to prepare for their 'hellos'. I would like them to feel empowered through their experiences. The Moving Booklet is my own creation, which I set out to improve each year, and give to my students who move during or at the end of the school year.

I am grateful for all the literature and resources currently available to parents and educators to guide children through the challenges of a global move. However, there is very little literature available to these children themselves. With this book, I hope to give younger TCKs a story they can identify with while they experience their own challenging move. I would also like to encourage them to enjoy a transition in life that can be a rewarding journey. Although targeted at a younger TCK audience, I also hope to reach out to parents and educators of TCKs.

This fictional 'memoir' is about the experiences of a ten-year-old girl and her teddy bear who have to move yet again. During the different stages of another relocation, Emma's search for home takes root. As the chapters alternate between Emma's point of view and that of her bear, Emma is emotionally torn, whereas B, her bear, serves as the wiser and more experienced voice of reason.

I hope you will enjoy their journey.

Valérie Besanceney
Gryon, Switzerland
www.valeriebesanceney.com
www.facebook.com/besanceneyvalerie

1

Moving Again

"Sweetheart, there's something we need to talk about as a family," Mom says, trying to sound casual, serving Emma her lamb cutlet.

The delicious looking meat is sitting on her plate, along with her favorite little tomatoes, rice and green beans. This yummy meal is usually only served at special occasions. Instead of loading her fork hungrily, Emma pauses with her knife in midair while she goes through a checklist of possible special occasions. She can't think of any.

"Is it bad?" Emma asks, wondering if this is a trap and the meal is supposed to compensate for something.

"Not at all, sweetie. It's actually rather exciting," Mom replies, smiling and pouring a little more juice

1

into her daughter's glass. "Daan, why don't you tell her?" Mom sits down and straightens the flowered napkin on her lap. She gives Emma's father a look that indicates a shared secret. He winks back at Mom.

Emma watches this exchange. "Well? What is it?" she asks impatiently and eagerly takes her first bite.

Dad puts his hands on the edge of the dark oak table and taps his fingers on the wood. "The bank asked us if we would like to relocate to Luxembourg and we said 'yes'," he says, expecting an emotional reaction from Emma. Either she'll be thrilled, furious, or something in between.

"What? Again? We are moving *again*?" Emma lays down her knife and fork. She is not hungry any more. Instantly, she feels tears welling up in her eyes and she starts to bite her bottom lip.

"We know it will be hard for you to leave your friends and school, but it will be exciting, sweetie," Mom says. "I promise."

Exciting, Emma thinks. *Right. Taking off for a vacation to an exotic island is exciting. Getting a present you've been wanting for a long time is exciting. Having a little brother or sister finally join the family would be exciting. Moving is not exciting at all!*

"We've only just moved back here!" Emma puts her hands on her armrest and leans back feeling defeated and cheated. She stares at their dog Gypsy's tail coming out from underneath the table, trying hard not to cry.

"It's been three years, darling," Mom responds with a look that gently tells her to stop exaggerating.

Three years, Emma thinks to herself, *three years it took me to settle back into this life in the Netherlands!* When she was five years old, the family had moved from their little cottage in the Dutch farm fields to a much bigger town in Switzerland. Then when she was seven, they suddenly moved back to the Netherlands. Mom was right, it was already three years ago, but it sure didn't feel like that long to Emma.

"It's a new challenge," Dad adds, "and you'll see, it'll be a wonderful opportunity for you to experience another country. You will go to an international school, meet new friends, be able to practice your English again—"

"What about Gypsy?" Emma interrupts him. She isn't ready to think about all the things she should look forward to. Her head is too full of thoughts about what she will miss.

"He'll come of course," Mom replies calmly.

"We wouldn't leave him behind, now would we?" Dad assures her while petting the big brown sheepdog now lying near his feet.

"Emma," her mother continues, "it's only a five hour drive from Stolwijk. We aren't moving to the other side of the planet."

Emma doesn't answer. She looks down at the way her mint sauce is starting to look rather brown as the lamb juice soaks into it. Again, she tries hard to swallow the big lump in her throat. Dad looks at Emma and then at Mom.

"Sophia?" he says quietly, as if he is begging her to help him out. He shrugs his shoulders a little and turns the corners of his mouth into an upside down smile in the way he always does when he is at a loss for words. He hates seeing Emma unhappy, but he isn't sure what to say to make it better for her.

"What is it, sweetie?" Mom asks Emma, reaching over to stroke her hair. It seems as if no one is very hungry anymore.

"I just started to like it here," Emma quietly whispers. "I don't want to move. Not now."

"We understand you are happy here, but—" Dad tries.

"No, you don't! You don't understand anything. If you did, you wouldn't make me move again! And it's not just my friends and school that are hard to leave, it's everything!" Emma blurts.

"Emma, we love you. Of course we want to do what's best for you, but we have decided that this is the best thing for us as a family," Mom calmly explains.

"What about me? Why don't I get a say in this? I am ten years old, I'm not a baby anymore!" Emma squeaks, slapping her right hand on the table and wondering why her voice deserts her when she needs it most.

"Look, we know we are putting you in a difficult situation, but if it weren't Luxembourg it would have been another place. Trust me, there have been some places we said 'no' to simply because we knew it wouldn't be a good place for you to grow up." Dad stabs a bean with his fork.

"Why didn't you tell me about the other places?" Emma asks, taking a big sip of juice, hoping it might calm her down a little.

"Because we don't want you to worry about every possible place we *could* end up in. Emma, you know my job means we will move around. Unfortunately, it's not always up to me how long we stay somewhere. I only get a final say in *where* we go. And Luxembourg seems like the best option for all of us right now."

Maybe for you, but not for me, Emma thinks.

Mom sighs. "We promise you'll be able to help decide on lots of important things that will be part of the move."

"Like what?"

"You can give us your opinion about the different schools you could go to and which house we'll choose to live in," Dad suggests.

"How long will we be there?" Emma's voice shrinks to a whisper the sadder she becomes.

"We can't be sure. Perhaps two, maybe three years," Dad answers, running his hand over his face in a way that shows he is getting tired.

"Maybe even longer," Mom adds cheerfully, but Emma can tell from the sound of her voice she is just saying that to make her feel better. "Emma, try to eat a little something." Mom urges with a pleading look.

Emma cuts a piece of meat off and adds a small tomato to her fork. Slowly she starts to chew her food, still thinking about the things she will miss. She is in fourth grade now and the most exciting thing about moving up to fifth grade is that her parents were going to allow her to bike to school with her friends, all by herself. When they move, she might never get to bike to school!

"What about my bike, can I bring it?"

"Of course!" Mom says.

"Will I be able to bike to school?"

Dad glances at Mom. Emma is starting to get irritated by the knowing looks passing between them.

"You know, Emma, there are no mountains like the ones we had in Switzerland, but it is very hilly in Luxembourg. It would be tough for you to bike to school and back every day. Mom and I will probably have to drive you."

"Don't worry, you'll still have plenty of opportunities to ride your bike," Mom says gently.

"You'll probably get to use those gears a whole lot there," Dad adds with an encouraging look.

Biking everywhere is one of the best things about living in the Netherlands. Her new bike was supposed to take her anywhere without needing Mom and

Dad for rides. Her parents had always promised her that she would be allowed to pick out a new bike for her tenth birthday. Emma had hardly been able to contain her excitement. She had pleaded for one with gears. Even though the Netherlands is as flat as a pancake, the idea of having gears seemed very grown up. Finally, on her birthday in November, her parents had taken her to the small local bicycle store in town. Even though it was a tiny shop, they seemed to have every type of bike you could imagine.

Emma picked out a beautiful white bike. It had six gears, big wide pedals, and tires that could take her through any kind of terrain, come rain or shine. There were straps to hold her backpack safely on the rack and it had a dynamo powered front light that only needed a little tap by the wheel to switch it on. She loved everything about it and felt herself grow a few inches taller when she rode it.

"You'll be able to use it for years," Dad had jokingly said. Although she was a hundred percent Dutch by blood, Emma was incredibly short for a Dutch girl. Mom and Dad always liked to tease her that she would never grow out of anything quickly.

Little did Emma know then that the days of biking to school were never even going to happen. Moving means she will be stuck in her parents' car again. Emma sees herself staring out of the window while Mom asks dull questions about her day.

Emma looks down at her meal. She has completely lost her appetite and just wants to be alone. She puts down her knife and fork together on her plate.

"When do we leave?" she asks in a quiet voice.

"Not until the summer, sweetie. There are still six weeks left before the end of the school year. And once the summer vacation starts, we'll be here for a couple of weeks before we move. Plenty of time to say your goodbyes." Mom sounds much too chirpy to Emma.

"May I be excused?" Emma gets up and leaves the dinner table without really waiting for the answer. She feels bad that she hasn't finished the meal Mom had prepared her. Then again, she'd probably only fixed her favorite out of guilt anyway, so what did it matter?

"Emma, please come back," Mom pleads.

Emma hears Dad murmur, "Let her be for a while. She probably just needs to digest this news on her own."

As Emma stomps up the stairs, B feels the vibrations of her footsteps as she comes up to her room. The door flings open so fast that B feels the wind ruffle his fur before Emma slams it shut behind her.

"Just because you guys love mountains and hills, doesn't mean I do," she growls before flinging herself on her bed, grabbing B, and starting to cry.

"I don't want to go," B hears Emma sob, as her tears begin to seep into his face.

"Home! I just want to be home," Emma keeps saying and presses her face deeper into B.

B is used to having the life squeezed out of him and braces himself for another really big squish. He lets Emma vent silently. After all, teddy bears are known to be wonderful listeners, always there to give nothing but comfort.

Be home. B listens to the word 'be' that is pronounced exactly the same way as his name. When Emma was little she couldn't pronounce the word 'bear' and somehow 'B' stuck.

"You know what I mean? I just want to be home!" Emma whispers into his ear, now covered with her snot and tears.

Of course I do, B wants to tell her. *What you mean to say is: I just want to belong somewhere. Being at home does not necessarily have anything to do with where you are, but everything to do with where you belong.*

Not only does B listen really well, but he can also translate Emma's confused feelings into clearer thoughts.

Too bad she never learned to listen to me though, B grumbles to himself.

"It's just ... I mean ... Oh, I don't know. Mom and Dad are Dutch and everyone else in the family lives here, and I guess I'm Dutch, but I don't always feel like I am ... And we already moved once before, and I still miss my friends from Zurich ... And I don't want to lose my friends here ... And what if I don't fit in?" Emma rambles on.

B tries to make sense of all her gibberish. *We're moving? Yippee!* B loves a good adventure and gives himself a minute to process this wonderful news before he turns his attention back to Emma.

She always tries so hard to figure out where home is and what it means to her. B thinks back to previous moves. *Remember when we had just moved to Switzerland?* B wants to ask her. *For the first few weeks you clung to me every evening, telling me all your fears about not fitting in, not understanding the language, not making friends easily. But then you learned to speak English and German! You made new friends! And you fit right in! It just takes time.* He has a feeling Emma is going to keep him busy with her thoughts and worries for a while, this time too.

"... I guess I will make new friends eventually," his friend continues.

Of course you will! And then you'll stop talking to me again, B wants to remind her. Somehow, Emma never told him much about her thoughts when she was feeling happy. Once she was settled into life in Zurich, he was just used as a pillow for ages. It was only when they moved back to the Netherlands that he became her confidant again.

Even B had realized there hadn't been much to come *back* to, apart from the house. Emma was older and had to attend a different school. Her best friend from preschool had moved to another town. She didn't really know how to read or write in Dutch as well as the other kids in her class. Nothing about 'home' turned out to be the same home she had left before moving to Switzerland.

"... But I don't want to move again!" Emma wipes her runny nose on his thinning tummy. B longs to hold her tight and tell her everything will be all right. From watching the fun Emma had in every country they had lived in or traveled to, he knows that change always brings along exciting new experiences.

2

The Good and The Bad

EMMA THINKS ABOUT THE CONVERSATION AT THE dinner table, rolls over to lie on her back and sighs. She isn't sure how she feels at all. Even though she is definitely feeling a little bit excited at the prospect of moving to another country again, that is quickly drowned by feelings of guilt and anger. She doesn't think it's right to feel excited, because more than anything she is upset to leave this life behind.

As she looks around her room, she feels sad that soon it will no longer be her room. Immediately, Emma feels guilty. Surely, her things are the last things she should worry or be sad about? Truth is that she'd just redecorated it after the fire last year. Emma had been ready to give her small but cozy room a more grownup look. When her room caught fire in a storm, it had given her the perfect opportunity to do a total makeover, albeit in a slightly brutal way. She had gotten used to her new space quickly. Where there once was a wooden dollhouse, there now sits a little white couch with two brightly patterned pillows. Next to it stands the big, broad white desk with its matching pink drawers she put together with Dad. Emma knows she can probably take it all with her, but she simply doesn't want it to go somewhere else. It looks perfect in *this* room.

"Hoohoo, hoohoo."

Emma turns her head toward her small bedroom window, and looks at Pim, Pam, and Pom. The three owls that made their home in the trees right outside her bedroom window have almost become like pets. Pom has an almost all black face, Pam has brownish raccoon-like eyes and Pim is the big fat one.

"Now that I can finally tell the difference between them, we have to leave," Emma complains with a sigh, rubbing her eyes with the base of her palms. At least Gypsy is allowed to come with them.

She sits up on her bed and grabs the heavy atlas off the pink bookshelf above her bed. *Maatje*, her grandmother who died much too early, had given it to her two years ago as a Christmas gift. Emma loves leafing through it and tracing routes between cities with her index finger. Somehow it feels more real to her than looking at an online map. She looks up Luxembourg.

"I guess Mom is right, it's not that far," she murmurs to B, tracing the distance between Amsterdam in the Netherlands to Luxembourg, the capital of Luxembourg. Below the map a short description reads 'A country so small that you can drive through it within an hour, yet they speak three different languages'.

"At least I can practice my German again," Emma glances a little further south on the map of Western Europe at the city of Zurich.

"We'll be halfway back to Switzerland," she says in a flat voice to B. Emma knows her parents would love to move back to Switzerland, but apparently that wasn't an option this time around. Maybe next time. Just the thought of yet *another* move after Luxembourg is enough to bring back that big lump in her throat.

Why can't we be a normal *family like everyone else? Why can't I live in one house all my life? Why do we have to keep moving? Surely Dad can get a better job here in Amsterdam, can't he?*

A thought comes to Emma. She reaches for her journal underneath a pile of books on the floor next to her bed. From the drawer in her nightstand she grabs her favorite pen, the one with the little cow on top that moves up and down as she writes. Perhaps she can convince her parents this whole move is a bad decision. Dad always tells her to weigh up the good and the bad sides before making any decision. He loves creating 'pros and cons' lists.

"Whenever you aren't sure what to do about a situation, you should make two lists side by side. On one list you write down all the good things, the 'pros', and on the other side, the 'cons', the bad things," he explained to her once. "And when one list is longer than the other you'll know what decision to make."

She writes a big T in the middle of the page to divide up the space. On the left side she'll write her pros and on the right side her cons. Emma sets to work, the little cow bobbing along happily as she makes her list. This is what she writes:

Pros	Cons
New friends	Saying goodbye to friends
New school	Saying goodbye to school
New house (bigger room?)	Saying goodbye to house
Gypsy can come	Leaving Owls
	No more tennis and swimming?
	Will I find new friends?
	Will I fit into the new international school?
	Do I still speak English well enough?
	Where do I belong?

Emma contemplates her cons list. So many goodbyes and uncertainties. The pros are not making her feel any better. She takes another look at her questions. Questions she won't find the answers to until she gets there.

"Hmmph, this won't really work to convince my parents," Emma says, sighing to B. She takes the elastic band around her wrist and ties her blond hair into a bun on top of her head. Picking up her pen, she starts doodling little waves around her list. Her pen moves up and down as she follows the crest of each wave. While she draws, it dawns on Emma that the list helps her understand her questions about moving better. Still, it leaves her with that nervous feeling deep down inside.

She stares at the waves and begins to think of swimming. Emma loves to swim, but always hates that first dive into the cold water. The only reason she manages to tough it through that freezing first plunge, is that terrific feeling of the water rushing past her body as she glides through it.

Thinking about all the pros and cons is not going to help me get through this. I just need to dive in and keep swimming. Maybe I will start liking it after a few strokes?

She glances back at the waves around her list. She feels a little like a wave herself, constantly moving in and away. Her eyes linger on the word 'goodbye'.

Grabbing B, she starts whispering to him.

"Saying my goodbyes will hurt, but leaving without saying them will probably hurt more." She'll never be able to go through the pros side of the list without dealing with the cons first. Like with swimming. You have to deal with the cold jump in, and then you can enjoy the water.

Before diving into this new adventure, she needs to make sure she can properly say goodbye to this part of her life. She turns to a crispy new page in her journal and starts writing another list. This time it is a 'to do' list:

* Make sure to say goodbye to everyone and everything
* Throw a goodbye party
* Take tons of pictures
* Make sure to have everyone's email address/ Skype name

Emma lies down on her bed again, facing the ceiling, and closes her eyes. She knows she will add more to her list later. Shutting her eyes real tight, she lets her eyes slip into screensaver mode, constantly changing into meaningless images. She loves doing this. It reminds her of the kaleidoscope with many different colored beads that she used to have.

Suddenly Emma realizes home will never ever be one place. It will be constantly moving. Like the waves, like the beads in the kaleidoscope. *Will there ever be one single place I can really call home? Or will I always move through different places like a wave? In and out with the tide, constantly cradled between the ebb and flow?*

"Wherever home is," she whispers to B and hugs him tightly, "will you come with me?"

Even though she is getting much too old for a teddy bear, she can't bear the thought of ever leaving him behind. After all, you simply don't grow out of things you love.

Of course I'll come with you. It's not like I have a choice, B thinks. He finds it very irritating when she asks him questions to which his answers are completely irrelevant.

He thinks that Emma is being slightly overdramatic about the whole situation, but deep down, home is something he still struggles with a little too. The uncertainty of not knowing where you are going is always a bit frightening, but B definitely feels it's better than staying in one place. If only there were a way for him to tell Emma about his own personal journey and how he had learned to accept things always change. How he longs to help her and to ease her pain, but Emma needs to make this journey herself.

"How old is B?" Emma would often ask her parents when she was little.

"Just as old as you are, Emma, and then some," they would answer.

Truthfully, before B had met Emma, his life had been extremely boring, but he is not exactly sure how long that time had been.

"Where was he born?" would be her next question.

"In Ireland, sweetie, where a friend of your dad bought him for you the day you were born," Mom would explain.

"But who was his mommy?"

This question never seemed to be answered clearly, because no one knew the answer. B assumed that at some point someone created him, but luckily he has no recollection of it. His maker had once taken the time to put his round, beige head together, to sew two little bright orange eyes on his head, to use some black yarn for his button nose, and some red yarn for his wise smile.

Although this part of him had been made with care, the rest of his body was odd. More like an afterthought. Instead of being stuffed with cuddly cotton or wool, he was left with an empty belly with a zipper at the bottom.

Come to think of it, he really isn't much of a teddy bear. His fur is beige and scraggly, not like the plush short hair which comes in many different colors. If he hadn't managed to live with this odd body for so long, he'd have thought it must have been a joke!

If he could have had a say in the matter, he probably would have put himself together quite differently. *No point in wishing for things that can't be changed,* he often tells himself.

"I wish I had curly hair instead of straight hair ... I wish I had brown hair ... I wish I was taller ... I wish I had more freckles ..." Emma would sometimes complain to him. B thinks this is a waste of wishing. After all, it's each of our little idiosyncrasies that makes us unique. He has learned to enjoy being 'one of a kind'.

His creator sold him to an old Irish shopkeeper. B ended up, for what seemed forever, on the dusty third shelf of a dark, narrow toyshop in Dublin. The shelf was just a little too high for most children to reach and too low for most adults to notice.

Emma might think staying in one place seems very appealing, but B cannot imagine having stayed on that shelf for much longer without losing his sense of humor forever.

"What about this one?" a mother once said to her little boy as she held B up to him.

"No, he's ugly. He isn't even stuffed!" the boy had replied as he disapprovingly squished the newspaper that the shopkeeper had put into B's belly.

"It's not your outside, but what's inside of you that really matters," he often hears Sophia tell Emma.

The truth is though, it's the outside that always gets judged first. When you are for sale on a shelf, no one has the time to get to know what you are like on the inside.

Every now and then, a child would pick B up from the shelf. When his or her attention was diverted to one of the other better looking, softer or bigger bears, he would be put down again absentmindedly – often upside down or sideways. This would infuriate him. He'd have to stare at the ceiling, or another toy, or even worse, the rough wood of the shelf. Frequently he would remain in an uncomfortable position until the shopkeeper was ready to close shop for the evening and quickly rearranged the toys neatly again. Days would pass and no one would show interest in him. This made him sad, but B knew there was nothing he could do about it. He quietly and stoically accepted his extended shelf life.

All B knows is that the day he was picked from that shelf was the day he felt as if his life had finally started. Like everything in his life, it hadn't been his choice, but life has a funny way of choosing for you sometimes.

You may not like what's happening to you. It may be beyond your control. What you can do, Emma, is choose how you deal with it, B wishes he could tell his sad and scared friend.

3

Where is Home?

EMMA FINALLY GETS UP AND STARTS GETTING HERSELF ready for bed. She changes into her pajamas – a T-shirt a friend had given her with about 16 different types of smiley faces on it. One for every mood. Right now, she identifies mostly with the unhappy face on the left corner of her stomach. She walks to the bathroom, and as she starts brushing her teeth, she hears Mom's footsteps on the stairs. She is furious with her parents, but she knows she won't be able to stay angry for very long.

Emma continues to brush her teeth a little longer than necessary. When she walks back into her room, Mom is waiting for her on the bed and holding B. Gypsy follows Emma into her room and is making himself comfortable at the foot of her bed.

"How are you feeling, Emma?" Mom asks, stroking B's head and putting him down on Emma's pillow.

"I don't know." Emma sits down next to Gypsy. She puts her arms around his soft neck and leans her head against his.

"Are you still very upset with us?"

"No. Yes. No and yes. I don't know!" Emma says with an irritated voice as she lifts her head off Gypsy and sits on the floor cross-legged. Frustrated with her emotions, she is trying hard not to be childish about the prospect of moving again. At the same time she just wants to curl up on Mom's lap and cry. She looks at her mother. "Where is home? I mean, like, where is it for you?"

"Well, at first it was in the Netherlands because I was born here. But then I used to think Suriname was home because that's where I spent most of my life as a little girl. Then the Netherlands became home again. Now home is wherever you and Daddy are. What about you, where do you think home is for you?"

"I don't know anymore. I know it's where you guys are, but it's also in different places. Part of it's in Zurich. Another part of it is this house the first time we lived here. Since we've been back it's become home again, but not in the same way." Emma's voice is starting to quaver again. "Home is just always changing."

"You know, sweetheart, I get that moving around is tough on you, but home doesn't have to be one place. You'll have to find out for yourself what it means for you. And once you find it, you can always take it with you. Wherever you go."

"So how do you take home with you?" Emma kisses Gypsy on the forehead and sits next to Mom on the bed.

Mom throws her arm around Emma and pulls her close. "It's like when I tell you stories about when I was a little girl. All those stories go with me no matter where I am, so that part of 'my home' is always close to me."

Emma hugs Mom and slips under the covers.

"Get a good night's rest, sweetie." Mom pulls the covers over her daughter and tucks her in. She sits down in the chair next to Emma's bed.

Turning on to her side to face Mom, Emma squeezes her mother's hand. Three quick squeezes. She gets three quick squeezes back. Two long, two short. Three short, two long. The squeezes don't mean anything in themselves, but the trick is for them to duplicate the exact number of squeezes, both in length and strength. It's a little game between the two of them, a reassurance that everything will be all right.

"Tell me one more story." Emma has heard them over and over, but she can never get enough of Mom's stories. Mom has told them for as long as she can remember. She often tells stories about her travels as a flight attendant, but Emma's favorites are the ones about her adventures growing up in the wild jungle of South America.

"Which one?" her mother asks her.

"Tell me about the time you went waterskiing with the caimans."

"All right then, but after that you must go to sleep."

"Promise." Emma squeezes Mom's hand real tight, letting her know she means to keep her promise.

"When we lived in Suriname, your grandfather's idea of an ideal vacation would be to take your uncles and me to the jungle."

Emma had been learning more about geography and suddenly thinks it is odd that they would always go to the jungle on vacation.

"Why didn't you go to the beach? Isn't Suriname next to the ocean?"

"Your uncles, *oom* Jan and *oom* Willem, and I would have much rather gone to the beach or on a vacation to the Caribbean, but your *Paatje* insisted we sleep in hammocks and learn to enjoy and survive in nature."

"What about *Maatje* and *oom* Roel? Would they come, too?"

"No, your grandmother usually stayed home with your youngest uncle. Anyway, we would take the little motorboat and cruise down the narrow, brown, murky river taking turns on big old wooden waterskis.

We knew there were piranhas and caimans living in the dark water, and this was the only fun activity we could do without staying in the water for too long. Your uncles would love nothing more than to get a good speed, and then, when I would least expect it, slow the boat down. I would feel my body slowly sinking into the water. Meanwhile the caimans, which had been sunbathing quite harmlessly on the riverbanks, would suddenly start moving. Sometimes their curiosity got the better of them and their scaly bodies would disappear into the water. That's when your uncles would rev up the motor again and I'd be so grateful to get back on top of the water! I certainly learned how to waterski very well, very quickly."

Emma chuckles at Mom and imagines the caimans swimming towards her as she gets pulled out of the water, the engine roaring through the jungle.

"And what happened again, that one time with the snake?" Emma asked.

"Ah, the snake … I was moving forward on the waterskis and as I looked up I saw a very big snake ahead of me slowly moving down a branch hanging right over the spot in the river I needed to cross. I knew if I would slow down or fall right underneath him, the snake might get frightened by my sudden movement and attack. Luckily, your Uncle Jan saw it as well, and he made sure he went full speed ahead. I managed to steer right past the snake."

"And tell me again how your toe got bit open by a piranha?"

"Sweetheart, another time," Mom looks at her watch. "You must go to sleep now."

"Then just tell me about Aunt Sidonia." Aunt Sidonia was the caiman Mom and her brothers took home as a pet and hid in the washing machine. They would sit on the top of the stairs waiting for *Maatje's* reaction when she opened the lid to the washing machine. "Please."

"Another night, sweetheart. I don't want to run out of stories this early in the week. How about 'Fourteen Angels' before you fall asleep?" Mom asks, stroking Emma's forehead.

Emma yawns, nodding her head 'yes'. *Maatje* had always recited the little verse of 'Fourteen Angels' to her before she went to sleep whenever she spent the night at her house. Just last year she passed away, and Emma misses her terribly. She was the only grandparent she had ever really known and by far the most wonderful grandmother she could imagine having. Emma didn't really believe in angels, but the idea of *Maatje* watching over her in her sleep comforted her. Although she never had to struggle with caimans and snakes, Emma does have the bad habit of falling into deep dreams that sometimes trouble her for days.

Tucking B under her head, Emma repeats after Mom:

"When at night I go to sleep,
Fourteen angels watch do keep:
Two my head are guarding,
Two my feet are guiding,
Two are on my right hand,
Two are on my left hand.
Two who warmly cover,
Two who o'er me hover,
Two to whom 'tis given,
To guide my steps to heaven."

Mom strokes her head one last time, and then gets up and turns the light off.

"Mom?"

"Yes, sweetie?"

"Can I tell everyone about the move already?"

"Yes, of course you can. We wanted to bring that up at dinner, but didn't get a chance." Mom leans against the doorpost. "You know, we wanted you to hear about the move first. We haven't told anybody else yet. We also waited to tell you until we were absolutely sure we're going. Now that we are, we can tell everyone else."

"Okay." Emma isn't looking forward to telling her friends she will be leaving. Partly because she is sad, but also because she is a little scared that they will be quite all right moving on without her.

"Let's talk more about it tomorrow, goodnight now, sleep well," Mom whispers. "Come on, Gypsy, let's go downstairs." The dog obediently gets up and follows Mom who leaves the door slightly open, just the way Emma likes it.

As she drifts off to sleep, Emma's thoughts are about the bear underneath her head, wondering whether he has any childhood memories she doesn't know about. She always likes to think B is her age, but perhaps he was born a long time before her. Slowly, she begins to slip into a dream, one where caimans chat with B about summer vacations and the piranhas show him how to find his way back home.

B ISN'T QUITE READY TO SLEEP. HE'S THINKING ABOUT how many nights he has spent lying squished underneath Emma's head. He now knows that he has always been destined to spend most of his life with Emma, and feels strongly about the nature of serendipity. Things always seem to happen for a reason and he can't help but think that this move is part of life's rich pattern, too.

However, he's also sure that the chance actions of others can change your life forever. B puts it down to a grain of randomness and a spoonful of fate that on a cold November morning in 2002 a man finally picked him up from the shelf.

What a funny looking thing, the man thought to himself, reading the attached card: 'A useful teddy bear to hold your pajamas'. *Hmmm, that might actually be a good gift,* he thought, remembering his own little boy. His son's pajamas somehow always ended up in a different spot every day, making it hard to find them come bedtime.

"This one please." The man handed the bear over to the shopkeeper with one hand as he reached for the wallet in his coat pocket with the other.

"Excellent choice, sir," the shopkeeper had replied as he held B up in the air and took a last good look at him. He wrapped him up with gift paper and handled him with more care than he had ever used before.

B likes to think that maybe the buyer had been smitten by his orange eyes. After all, he did remember looking at the man and thinking, *Pick me!* When he did, B's uncertain destination became a trail of inevitable, yet unforgettable, events into what he dared to call his life.

The trip from the shelf to the small bed in which he found himself a few days later, right next to baby Emma, had been terrible. His life so far had been tranquil and mostly motionless, but suddenly he found himself in all kinds of strange places.

Not long after they left the shop, the man tossed B into the corner of a big brown suitcase. A few hours later, the suitcase was thrown into the belly of a big airplane. The sounds of the engine had been deafening. Not knowing what was happening, and not being able to see anything through the wrapping paper, B had felt lonely and afraid. He wondered if he had foolishly convinced himself into believing that life outside the shop was going to be better.

B can't help but think about how badly he had wanted to move away from the shop and how much Emma doesn't want to move away right now. Sometimes the grass seems greener on the other side, but sometimes you just like the way the grass feels under your feet and you have no desire to walk anywhere else.

They say that it's not the destination but the journey that matters. If only he could help Emma enjoy this journey, and each moment of it for what it is. Then maybe she would also come to appreciate this next destination, without looking back or forward too much.

4

Never Give Up

THE NEXT MORNING, EMMA WAKES UP AND PULLS HER duvet around her. She is not in a hurry to get out of bed. She turns to her side, sees her journal on the floor next to the bed, and thinks about her pros and cons list. *I must dive in deep.* Mom is right about finding 'home', but Emma has a feeling she won't really know *what* and *where* and *who* home will be for a while.

Moving a lot means that home will constantly be taking on new shapes and colors just like a kaleidoscope, she reminds herself. Her eyes are still closed. *Maybe I should concentrate more on the* who *and* what *rather than the* where. Emma rubs the sleep out of her eyes and gets up out of bed.

"Emma, are you going to eat or are you going to

41

school without breakfast?" Mom asks while she is preparing Emma's cheese sandwich for lunch. Emma is staring at the corner of the kitchen table, her head resting on her left fist.

"Yes, I'll eat. Just a minute," she says, while she gives her head a quick shake to wake up.

"Listen, I was thinking about how we could make something that reminds you of here for your new room," Mom says.

"What, like a souvenir?"

"Yes! Just like souvenir. Did you know that souvenir means 'memory' or 'to remember' in French?"

"Okay, Mom, enough with the French lesson. What are you thinking exactly?" Emma says impatiently. She is not a morning person and Mom definitely is.

"Well, you could take the camera into school one day and take some pictures of your friends. We could turn them into a beautiful collage and print it as a poster."

Emma thinks for a moment while she pours some Brinta into a bowl and adds the warm milk that Mom put in front of her.

"What if I take the best photos and other little memories, like my ticket stubs to the theater and stickers of the tennis club and the pictures on my cork board and stick them all over my desk? I can cover it with something to harden it, like the glue we mixed with water the other day at school. That way my desk will have a whole new surface full of souvenirs," Emma says as she emphasizes the last word with a French accent. She can tell Mom is pleased that she used her idea to come up with an even better one.

"Brilliant idea, sweetie, go for it!" Mom breaks into a smile. "Let me grab the camera for you. Now, eat your breakfast!"

Emma starts gulping her porridge and washes it down with a glass of orange juice. She looks inside her lunch box and sees the usual cheese sandwich, apple, and yogurt. *What kind of lunch will I be eating in Luxembourg? Will Mom pack different lunches over there?* She hopes not, because cheese sandwiches are the best. Suddenly a feeling of panic overwhelms her.

"Mom, do they sell Dutch cheese in Luxembourg?" she asks, as she puts her lunchbox in her school bag. Mom is rummaging through the top drawer of the cabinet by the kitchen door. She hands the camera to Emma.

"Here you go. Come on, we'll be late for school if we don't leave now. What did you say about Dutch cheese?" she asks, grabbing her coat and the car keys.

"*Goudse kaas.* Do you think they'll have it in Luxembourg?" Emma moves her chair back and puts her empty bowl in the dishwasher.

"Of course they will, and if not, we'll stock up whenever we're back or someone visits." Mom hands Emma her school bag. "You know, there might be some new cheeses to try there that you'll really like."

"Sometimes when you really love something, you don't want to try something else though." Emma grabs her thin fleece to ward off the early morning chill.

"Sure. Sometimes you're lucky enough to have a choice. Other times not." Mom looks thoughtful and rattles her car keys.

Emma slides her arms into the sleeves of her fleece and finds herself thinking of B and how she almost lost him forever. "Like with the fire, Mom. Everyone tried to give me new stuffed animals trying to replace B, but all I wanted was B."

"I know, sweetie." Mom gently pushes Emma towards the front door. Gypsy follows them to the car and hops straight to his regular spot in the backseat of their old faithful hatchback, right next to Emma.

Once they are sitting in the car, Emma presses on, "If we look hard enough, I'm sure we can find Gouda cheese in Luxembourg." The one thing she learned from the fire is that you should never give up looking for something you love.

LESS THAN A YEAR AGO, EMMA HAD BEEN BRAVE ENOUGH to leave B at home during a weekend field trip with her class.

"I don't want to lose him at camp," she had told her parents, but B suspected that she had not wanted her friends to know she still slept with her teddy bear. B hadn't minded very much, and welcomed the relief, for a couple of nights, from being squeezed under her head or dropped onto the floor while she slept.

The next day, B had felt the summer heat rising in the little room right underneath the thatched roof.

"Let's get some fresh air in here!" Sophia said. She had come into Emma's room and opened a window to let some breeze come through, but the heat had been stifling. The sun had set and an impending storm was in the air. B could smell the rain coming. Suddenly thunder started to rumble and roll over the wide farm fields around them, and zig-zags of lightning flashed in the black clouds overhead. B wondered how Emma was doing. She hated thunderstorms.

All of a sudden he felt the bed shudder before an earsplitting crack followed by a deafening roar stormed through the room. After a few seconds, Gypsy started barking loudly before B recognized the familiar steps of Sophia sprinting up the stairs once again. As she opened Emma's door, she stopped in her tracks, raised her face and sniffed the air. B had thought it had started to smell a little smoky.

After one quick glance through the window, Sophia closed the door firmly and quickly went downstairs again. Smoke started filling the room and B had felt a sense of panic rise inside his skinny tummy. Soon he wasn't able to see anything anymore. Unlike humans, he didn't need air to breathe but he had felt the room getting hotter and hotter. He feared the worst. *Please come back, please,* he silently begged Sophia.

After what seemed an eternity, B heard another rush of steps on the stairs. Before he knew it, three firefighters in black uniforms stormed into Emma's room. He had not been able to see them right away, but as they approached the bed he noticed one of the men spraying water with a big hose. The water seeped into his body. It was freezing!

"Throw the mattress out of the window *now*!" the one with the hose screamed. The other two men grabbed the mattress right off the bed and doubled it over with all their might. B felt himself being squeezed together harder than Emma ever had the strength to do. What little there was left of the stuffing in his head was compressed even more. He had felt like those flat puppets Emma would sometimes cut out of her magazines.

Suddenly his body flew through the air and his head whooshed back into shape. Bang! He landed with a thud on the hard earth. A second later there was an even louder crash as the mattress landed right on top of him. Whump! His face was forced into a layer of dirt. With one orange eye he noticed how he had landed only feet away from the little canal next to the house. As he lay there under the mattress, pieces of furniture were thrown on top of him, forcing the air right out of him. For the first time ever, B had been scared for his life.

The storm blew over and the fire was put out. The battlefield of burned clothes, furniture, and Emma's belongings thrown from her bedroom window was left for another day.

B had missed being in Emma's comfortable room. Buried underneath a pile of soot and what remained of Emma's furniture, clothes and toys, he could not tell night from day. He missed the way Emma's activities marked his day with signs of normality. He had no idea how long he had been stuck out there. The only way he had known he was still alive was his yearning to get away from the mess. His orange eyes searched for some signs of light and life but found nothing.

Then he heard a familiar voice above his head. It was Emma's dad!

"Nothing has any true value except a teddy bear that my daughter is extremely attached to. I'm offering a reward for finding it. Considering the mess and dirt, it won't be easy, but please look out for two little orange eyes. Please," Daan pleaded, "this is the only thing that really matters."

The sweet sounds of those words had made B's heart do a little somersault. Waiting patiently, praying and hoping that his orange eyes had not been smothered with ash, he heard hands digging through the trash above and around him. Finally, after what had seemed an eternity but in reality had only been two days, a man picked him up, shook him around a little and wiped his face. He saw a small grin appearing on the stranger's face. Sophia leapt with joy at the sight of him and gave the stranger a big hug.

"You have no idea how happy she will be!"

B was surprised that Sophia still recognized him. After all, the man had handed over a black bear with dusty orange eyes. "I'm surprised we found him. It sure is a strange thing to look for after a fire. Usually it's the expensive stuff folks like to have back, but a bear ..."

"Trust me," Sophia had said, "you've just found the most valuable thing in that entire pile."

5

Telling Friends

"YOU KNOW, I NEVER GAVE UP ON B. I KNEW HE'D turn up," Emma says to Mom as they drive past the thatched farms on their road.

"Emma, may I remind you that you weren't the one who found B after the fire?" Mom says to her, looking at her in the rearview mirror.

"I know, but I'm so glad Dad made sure everyone kept looking for him. And if I ever experience a fire again, I will never stop looking for B!"

"Just make sure to tell the firefighters to throw out the mattress first," Mom says with a wink. Emma is glad they can joke about the fire now, because it definitely was not a happy experience for any of them.

As they do the usual round of carpool pickups, Emma decides to try out the news of their move on everyone joining them in the car.

"We're moving to Luxembourg!" she blurts out when Auke and Jorrit get in. They look at her a little confused. Clearly neither of them is awake yet.

"Cool," Auke mumbles, putting on his seatbelt in the passenger seat. "When?" he continues.

"Where is Luxembourg?" Jorrit asks, moving into the seat next to Emma. Gypsy, feeling cramped for space, dutifully jumps over the seat into the back of the hatchback.

After she answers these two simple questions, the two brothers start talking about the new video game they were playing the evening before. Emma tries to shrug off the feeling of being ignored and then breaks the news to Maaike when she joins them. Her friend, who is two years younger, looks at her sadly with her huge blue eyes.

"Oh, no! I'll really miss you!"

This makes Emma feel a little better, but then Maaike continues, "My dad went to Luxembourg for business a few weeks ago and said it was a really small, boring city. If my parents make us move again, I hope we will go to another exotic destination like Malaysia, where we were last. The best thing about Malaysia was ..."

Emma tunes out and starts staring out of the window. *I should have known better,* she thinks to herself, *Maaike always manages to turn anyone's news into a story about herself.* Emma looks at the endless flat farm fields outside as they drive to Gouda, the town where they go to elementary school. Rain starts to drizzle and Emma follows the slow movements of the windshield wipers. The others are all chattering about things that would usually interest Emma, but today she doesn't feel like joining in. By the time they get to school it's pouring with rain and everybody seems to have forgotten about Emma's big announcement. Hopefully, her other friends will be a little more interested in her life-changing news.

When Emma tries to follow the others out of the car, Mom gives her hand a quick squeeze and tells her to hold on a minute. Surprised, Emma leans back into the seat.

"You can't expect everyone else to be as interested in our news as we are, sweetie," Mom explains. "You're still here. They won't really realize what's happening until after you've left! Try to enjoy the time you have with your friends now. Don't worry about the move yet."

Emma just nods, thinking, *that's easy to say.* She tries to give Mom a brave smile back, closes the car door and puts on her backpack. She scans the playground and within seconds sees her group of friends sitting at their usual spot. She runs over and joins them underneath the bike shelter, protected from the rain.

"... and my brother says that the camp leaders let you chose who you want to sail the Optimists with," Femke just finishes her sentence. The summer sailing camp! With a sharp pain in her stomach, Emma realizes that sailing camp is probably not going to happen now they're moving. She decides to just spit out her news.

"Morning! I have some news. I'm moving at the end of the school year."

"What? Where to?" Charlotte asks excitedly. Charlotte has been her friend since preschool. Her family owns a small chalet in Switzerland that Emma and her parents rent for a vacation every year. Last summer Charlotte joined them on their hiking holiday.

"Luxembourg."

"Luxembourg? Why?" Mimi's face shows surprise and confusion and her tone sounds almost annoyed. Mimi had moved to Gouda from England when she was only six years old. Emma always feels like Mimi is her only friend in class who understands what it's like to move.

"I dunno. Banking I guess. It's for my dad's job. But we're not moving until the end of the school year," Emma hastily adds.

"Luxembourg, that is so *far*!" Femke's eyes are wide open.

"No, it's really not, it's only a five hour drive," Emma

hears herself snap back at Femke. She realizes she is trying to convince herself more than anyone else. And it's not Femke's fault she has always lived in the same place and doesn't travel a lot.

The morning bell rings. Everyone is busy grabbing their bags and walking towards the main entrance. Emma watches Mimi walk away, disappointed her friend doesn't give her any comforting response. It's like she is angry with Emma, even though she didn't do anything wrong. Charlotte comes up to her from behind and walks next to her.

"Hey, I'm really sorry you'll be leaving, Emma," she says with a warm smile on her face. "I really hope we'll still stay friends." This makes Emma feel a bit better, but she can't help wishing that Mimi would say the same.

Good thing today is a Wednesday, Emma thinks. Wednesdays are half days and she wants to go home already. Before she knows it though, she is working hard on her math problems. They make her forget the move for at least a little while.

At the start of morning recess Emma doesn't feel like going outside, instead she walks up to her teacher.

"*Juf* Anja?" Emma likes being able to call her Dutch teachers by the more informal teacher nicknames and first names.

"Yes, Emma, what is it?"

"Can I talk to you for a minute?"

"Of course, what's up?" she asks with her usual big smile. *Juf* Anja's smile always stands out more than any other teacher's, perhaps because she always wears bright red lipstick. Emma feels really lucky, because *Juf* Anja is definitely the nicest teacher she has ever had. She is also pretty cool. Somehow, many teachers have a boring 'look', but *Juf* Anja is really funky. She usually wears her long platinum blond hair down and always dresses in really colorful, happy outfits and high heels.

"I'm moving at the end of this school year," Emma says. "To Luxembourg," she adds.

"Oh, no! That's sad news for us!" *Juf* Anja makes a sad face that immediately softens into another smile. "How do you feel about it though? Are you excited?"

"Yes and no." Emma fiddles with the pencil sharpener on her teacher's desk.

"I can imagine that you're going through a bit of a roller coaster of feelings about it," *Juf* Anja says while looking at Emma questioningly.

That's exactly how I feel, Emma thinks to herself, *like I'm on a roller coaster. Excited, scared, happy, sad, up and down.* She nods.

"Hey kiddo, we're going to make your last few weeks here really good. We'll make sure you leave with tons of good memories! Why don't you tell me more about Luxembourg outside?" *Juf* Anja gently takes Emma by the hand. "I've never been there, I'd love to hear more."

They walk down to the playground and Emma is starting to feel a bit better about it all. She begins to tell *Juf* Anja everything she knows about Luxembourg so far.

At the end of the morning, Emma walks up to Mimi. Mimi is packing up her bag, and seems to be in a bit of a hurry.

"Do you want to come over to my house this afternoon?" Emma asks.

"No, I can't, I'm going to the dentist."

"Oh, that's too bad. Maybe this weekend?" Emma tries again hopefully.

"No, I don't think so, we're going to see my grandparents." Mimi looks away into the distance.

"Mimi, is something wrong? Are you mad at me?"

"Why didn't you tell me earlier?" Mimi doesn't look annoyed anymore, just sad.

"What do you mean earlier? About the move? I only found out last night!"

"But I'm your best friend ..." Mimi starts and that slightly angry look pops up again. Emma doesn't really understand why Mimi is getting angry.

"I'm sorry, Mimi, I wanted to tell everyone this morning," Emma says.

"Whatever. Go to your stupid Luxembourg. I don't care," Mimi mumbles under her breath and storms off.

Emma bites on her lip and feels tears welling up. *Great, I haven't even left yet, but I've already lost my best friend.* She grabs her bag from the floor and walks downstairs. As she comes down the stairs she sees Mom talking to Charlotte's mom.

"Hey Emma, I just heard your big news," Mrs Witte says as she walks up to them. Emma tries to force a smile.

"Are you excited?" Mrs Witte continues.

Emma glances at Mom, unsure what to answer. "I guess," she says.

"We're all still trying to wrap our heads around it, right Em?" Mom adds lightly as she rubs her hand over Emma's head. "Did you take any pictures today?"

"No, not yet."

"Pictures? What for?" Charlotte asks, joining them.

"I'm making a memory collage," Emma explains.

"Oh, I love taking pictures! Can I help you?" Charlotte offers.

"Sure, maybe tomorrow." Emma shrugs.

"Well, if there's anything we can do to help, just let us know," Mrs Witte says. "We have to run now though, Charlotte has violin lessons, see you tomorrow!"

"*Tot morgen!*" Emma and Charlotte say at the same time, which makes them giggle.

"All right, there is a smile at least. How did your day go?" Mom puts her arm around Emma as they walk towards the car. On Wednesdays, Emma never drives home with the carpool group because she and Mom usually go grocery shopping together.

"Mom, remember that one time when Daddy put the car in reverse to get B back?"

"Yes, of course." Mom moves her shoulders briskly as if to shake off the memory as quickly as Emma brought it up.

Emma imagines how her mother's heart skips a beat thinking about the fear she had felt driving backwards in the emergency lane. And yet ... "Sometimes, I wish I could do that, just drive back in reverse and fix things."

"Why do you say that?" Mom opens the car door for Emma. "Hold that answer, let me get in the car first."

Emma puts her seatbelt on and leans her head against the headrest.

"Okay, what's up?" Mom slides into her seat, clicks in her seatbelt, starts the engine and looks at Emma through the rearview mirror before driving out of the school's parking lot.

"I think Mimi is really angry at me, and ..." Emma feels a tear making its way down her cheek. "I wish I could go back and undo it."

"Emma, we can't always undo what's done. Sometimes things happen for a reason, even when we can't find a good reason at the time. What happened?"

Emma recounts her conversation with Mimi.

"I guess Mimi is upset that you're leaving," Mom says.

"She has a funny way of showing it," Emma whispers,

as she dries her cheeks with a tissue that Mom leans back and hands to her.

"Emma, Mimi probably felt a little hurt that she had to find out her best friend is leaving along with everyone else. Try to imagine how you would feel if it were the other way around."

Suddenly Emma understands. "It's just that ... I will miss Mimi so much! And Charlotte and Femke and Maaike ... and even Auke and Jorrit," she adds with an embarrassed chuckle between tears.

"I know, honey, but just because they can't come with you, it doesn't mean they can't come along in your heart. Remember, your heart will never fill up. Even if new people come into your heart, good old friends will stay there as well."

*

SOPHIA IS POKING HIM WITH A GREAT BIG NEEDLE.

Is this really necessary? B wants to ask her. *It's too early in the morning for this! Where is Emma when I need her?* He looks at the big round wooden clock hanging above the kitchen door. Almost nine thirty, which means Emma is at school.

"I should get some coffee going," Sophia puts B down and pulls the big old-fashioned coffee tin out of the cupboard, just as Auke's and Jorrit's mom walks in. B sighs to himself. Elizabeth is a very nice lady, but so loud! She comes around for a *bakkie koffie* at least once a week and he can't even hear himself think when she is there.

"Helloooo!" Elizabeth says a little too loudly. B listens to the ladies exchange the customary three kisses on the cheek: Smack, smack, smack! "How are you doing,

Sophia? I still can't believe you guys are moving again!" She puts down her bag and sits herself in one of the comfy armchairs.

"I know, neither can I." Sophia arranges some cookies in a small dish and sets them on the table. "But I'm good. Excited. Feel like I have a million things to take care of in the next few weeks. This morning seems to have flown by already. I was just doing a small repair on Emma's teddy bear." Sophia motions to B lying on the table, while she prepares two mugs of steaming coffee.

"Ah, I see." Elizabeth strokes the small piece of cloth covering a hole on B's neckline and the needle is nudged ever so slightly.

Owww! B hates it when he's being patched up, even if it's done out of love.

"Was there a zipper on this bear?" Elizabeth is holding B up, inspecting him and touching the tiny little piece of leftover zipper.

"Yes." Sophia laughs. "Emma enjoyed chewing on the coarse cloth it was attached to. By the time she was six, she almost managed to bite it off completely. Luckily, she had the good sense not to chomp on the metal part or to swallow any of it!"

"Sounds painful." Elizabeth grimaces and puts B back down.

Sure was! B wants to tell her.

"So, how is Emma handling the news about the move?" Elizabeth dips her cookie into the hot coffee.

"She was quite upset to start with, which we expected, but she's still taking it all in. She's definitely finding it difficult to say goodbye *again* ... And yesterday she had a bit of a fight with her friend Mimi. She mentioned how she wished she could reverse like Daan once did and 'fix the situation'."

"What on earth are you talking about?"

"Oh, this one time a few years ago, we were on our way to Switzerland to go skiing. Daan had just pulled back onto the *autobahn* after we had stopped for gas, when suddenly Emma, at the top of her lungs, wailed, 'Waaaaahhhh!' She started sobbing because she couldn't find B," Sophia picks up B and starts to finish sewing on the small piece of light pink cloth.

"'He must be in the car somewhere, don't worry, let's take a good look.' I tried to comfort her while frantically looking around for B. I've become almost as attached to this bear as Emma is." Sophia looks at him fondly.

"'Noooooooooo, he's nooooot ...' Emma spluttered back to me through her tears. She must have known she needed to tell the truth to get B back, but she also knew she was not going to do us a huge favor with this revelation. 'I ... I left him in the ba ... ba ... bathroom at the gas station.'"

"Oh no! So what did you do?" Elizabeth asks.

"Before I had time to realize what was happening, Daan had pulled into the emergency lane on the right hand side of the road. He slammed the car into reverse and pressed the gas pedal. We drove backwards for a few hundred meters in the emergency lane until we were back at the exit of the gas station."

"Yikes." Elizabeth gives a concerned look.

"I know. I was scared to death, but managed not to get angry. Once Daan had parked the car, I jumped out with Emma and we ran back to the bathrooms. When Emma saw B still sitting on the floor of the toilet stall where she had left him, she started crying, she was so relieved to find him."

I, on the other hand, had been furious, B thinks. He had been left behind! Not forgotten in the comfort of his own home, but left behind in a strange, dark, and awful smelling place. When Emma had shut the bathroom stall door, he had immediately experienced an overwhelming stomach-crunching feeling of loneliness combined with homesickness.

Unfamiliar footsteps of women and girls who walked into the stall had made him shudder. On the one hand, he was hoping for one of them to notice him flopped in the corner, just behind the toilet. On the other hand, he was terrified of what would happen if someone else did find him. After several years of being intensely squished and squashed, he didn't look so cute and cuddly anymore. Surely he wouldn't be welcomed with open arms into someone else's life at this point; certainly not if he was found on a dirty toilet floor. If anything, a worker might eventually find him, pick him up with those plastic gloves, and toss him in with all the other bathroom garbage.

It never came to that, but for the first time since meeting Emma, he had felt abandoned and unloved. He had started to doubt if she ever really cared about him. *How would she feel if I left her somewhere?* B knew this was impossible. *Maybe I'll hide from her on purpose sometime, just to spite her,* he had thought.

B knows how important his being there is to Emma. Just to be there. As wear and tear tugged at his body over the years, his value only seemed to increase in Emma's eyes. The longer he stayed with her, the more attached she became to him.

However, Emma usually seems to be oblivious to his general state of well-being. She always needs him when she is sad or lonely, but whenever she is happy, he is neglected. He knows she loves him, because she is always inconsolable when she cannot find him, but her forgetfulness and carelessness leave him in some appalling places. He definitely spent more time than he'd cared for at that German gas station.

After the *autobahn* incident, Emma began to be more cautious about taking B along everywhere she went. She stopped taking him out of the house altogether after a while, even for a short trip. Unfortunately, despite her concern, his safety was sometimes out of her hands.

6

The Moving Booklet

"EMMA, WOULD YOU COME HERE FOR A MINUTE, PLEASE?"

Emma walks into class and looks over at *Juf* Anja. She wonders if she did really badly on yesterday's math quiz.

"Good morning, *Juf* Anja," Emma says, walking up to her teacher's desk. *Juf* Anja is holding a small book bound together by a plastic ring spine. It has Emma's name on it.

"I'd like to give you something I made for you. It's a Moving Booklet."

Emma looks at her with quizzical, yet curious, eyes.

"It's filled with pages for you to write all about your moving experience. Kind of like a diary." *Juf* Anja opens it up. "Look, on the first page you can write about when you found out you were moving. I added a little map of Europe so you can show where you are going to, and here you can add a map of Luxembourg." *Juf* Anja points to the space next to the small map. "There are a few more pages, like these where you can note some of your favorite memories about your home, school, and friends. Anyway, why don't you have a look through it?"

Emma looks at the booklet and then at *Juf* Anja. Not quite sure what to say, she mumbles a 'thank you', looks up at her and smiles. She takes it to her desk to have a closer look.

Emma likes the Moving Booklet very much. Each page has a little frame around it made up of a moving truck and moving boxes. On the second page, there are lines for her to write on and spaces for her to draw pictures or add photographs of her family.

"What's that?" Charlotte asks as she sits down next to her.

"Um. A Moving Booklet. *Juf* Anja gave it to me."

"Cool, so where is Luxembourg?" she asks, inspecting the map on the first page.

Emma immediately finds the little country of Luxembourg and points it out to Charlotte.

As they continue to peruse the booklet, Emma sees that there are spaces to write down her thoughts and feelings about the move, what she is excited about, what she is scared about. There are pages to add photos of her house *now*, her room *now*, her school *now*, and her friends *now*. Immediately she imagines what those pages will look like.

"Oh, Emma! We need to take lots of pictures. Did you bring your camera to school today?" Charlotte asks.

"Yes, I did, I'll take it outside during recess."

"Cool!" Charlotte says, starting to look for something in her pencil case. Emma continues to turn the pages, and notices there are also pages for pictures and notes about all the things that will be new in her life. The *new* house, her *new* room, her *new* school, her *new* friends. Emma realizes she is starting to get a little excited just thinking about filling up these pages.

At the back there are spaces for her classmates to fill in their email address and to write her a personal message. When Mimi walks into the classroom, Emma gets up right away.

"Charlotte, excuse me, but I need to go speak to Mimi." Emma picks up the booklet and walks over to Mimi. "Hey, good morning, Mimi."

"Hi." Mimi seems a little less angry today.

"I know I upset you by not telling you first, and I am sorry about that, but I'd really like for you to be the first one to write in this booklet. *Juf* Anja made it for me."

Mimi looks at her a little surprised and then smiles meekly.

"Sure, no problem, Em." Mimi takes the booklet from her and flips through the pages. "It's going to look great once it's all filled in." Mimi looks at the frame with the title 'My closest friends'. In the frame is written 'Reserved for Mimi and Charlotte'.

Emma had scribbled that in while looking at it with Charlotte. All of a sudden Mimi gives Emma a big hug.

"Oh, I'm really going to miss you."

"I know. Me too. I mean, me too I will miss you. Not miss me. You know what I mean." They both start to laugh.

"Well, we've got about six more weeks, right? And what about sailing camp? You are coming with us, aren't you?" Mimi asks.

"Not sure, but I will definitely ask my parents again."

"Come on, class, everyone in their seats please, I'd like to take roll call," *Juf* Anja says. Emma quickly moves to her seat and listens to her classmates' names being called out alphabetically. She is one of the last. "Van Lier, Emma?"

"Present," Emma says with a grin. She is here now, present, and feeling much better about things.

B feels his head being squashed. Emma is sitting on her bed, leaning against the wall, and using B as her pillow. From the corner of his left orange eye, he can see she is working in some kind of booklet.

"Hmmm, my favorite thing about my room here," Emma says, taking a look around. She starts to write.

B has always wished that he could read and write. It is a human ability he's truly jealous of. After all, in his own humble opinion, he has led a very interesting life so far and wishes he could write some of it down. It would also help him share his thoughts with Emma. Or send a letter to his old friends in the Irish toyshop to let them know what has become of him.

At least he can be sure he is often written about. Not only does Emma mention him frequently in her journal, but Sophia had also written a great poem about him after the fire. Emma had read it to him many times and it always made him feel so much better about the horrendous experience. Mostly it was about how irreplaceable he had become to Emma and how no other stuffed animal, no matter how beautiful, cuddly, or big, *ever* managed to console Emma the way B did.

Emma sure seems to need some comforting these days. B looks at what she is writing. He cannot read it, but it looks like she's writing things down about her life here. And like in a book, she completes a chapter filled with memories. That way, when the time comes, she'll be ready to close it and start a new chapter.

B looks at the patchwork quilt that lies on her bed. One of Sophia's friends made it out of scraps of material from all the dresses and nightgowns and curtains that had ever been part of Emma's life – so far. The fire had taken away so many of those memories from Emma, but luckily Sophia had always saved these scraps in a big chest in the guest room. Thankfully, that room was on the other side of the house and had been untouched by the fire. Every time B lies underneath the quilt he feels like he is wrapped in the memories of not only Emma's, but also his own life. The warm blanket of memories feels familiar and safe.

"Hey, where do you think you're going?" Emma asks him as she leans forward and grabs him from behind her back. B had slid down from under her head and lost sight of what Emma was jotting down in her Moving Booklet.

Not going anywhere, B thinks. *I'll be with you for as long as you'll let me, Emma.*

She props him back up in the nape of her neck and continues to write.

B looks at the quilt again and hopes Emma can see how her quilt and photo collage will not only show her great memories, but also how incredibly rich her life is. He understands how tough moving can be, but he really hopes she doesn't lose sight of all the amazing people and experiences each move brings along.

7

Old and New Traditions

"Mom?" Emma walks into the kitchen with the camera Mom had given her a few weeks earlier. "Can you print these out for me?"

"How many pictures did you end up taking?" Mom asks, placing strawberries in a bowl.

"Hmmm, about 234," Emma responds, trying to sound casual, popping a strawberry into her mouth and realizing this is probably a few too many.

"Sweetie, do you think you could go through them and do a little editing? I love your idea of making a collage, but if we are going to try to fit 234 pictures onto your desk we'll need to make very small prints. And it will be very expensive."

"Sure, but only if you help me, because I kind of

want to keep them all." Emma gives the camera to Mom and sits next to her at the kitchen table. Mom connects it to her laptop and they begin flipping through the pictures.

"Great pictures, Em, but do you really need six of you, Charlotte, and Mimi? How about we pick two good ones?"

After an hour of looking through all the pictures, they decide to order 50 pictures in 9 x 13 cm size.

"Can I ask Charlotte to come over when we make the collage? She helped me out so much taking the pictures."

"Of course you can!" Mom is already busy placing the order online.

A few days later a thick envelope arrives in the mail with Emma's name on it.

"Mom! The pictures are here!" Emma yells, running into the kitchen.

"Wonderful!" Mom exclaims, walking up to the kitchen table where Emma is already laying them all out.

"May I call Charlotte and see if she can come over right now?"

"Sure, tell her that her mom is welcome to come over for a cup of coffee too." Mom hands Emma the phone.

Half an hour later Charlotte and her mom pull into the driveway. Mrs Witte and Mom busy themselves in the kitchen while Emma and Charlotte go up to Emma's room.

"I already cleared off my desk. Look, these are all the pictures." Emma hands Charlotte the thick stack.

"Wow! So many! Oh, this will be fun," Charlotte says, quickly scanning through the photos.

"Let's start with this one in the center," Emma says, pulling out one of Mimi, Charlotte and Emma making goofy faces.

"Perfect, and what about this next one to it?" Charlotte hands Emma one of the whole class and *Juf* Anja standing in the playground.

It takes them about two hours to arrange all the pictures. With pinking shears they give some of them zigzag edges. Finally, they add some stickers, old ticket stubs, and cutout quotes from magazines as a background and to fill in any gaps.

"Do you remember how to make that Mod Podge type of glue we used at school? You know, the glue that leaves a sealed surface on top of the pictures?" Emma asks Charlotte.

"I think it was two units of normal white glue to one unit of water, but maybe we should see if we can check it online. Let me go ask." Charlotte runs down the stairs.

Meanwhile Emma looks at the collage and smiles.

She loves it! Two minutes later Charlotte is back with both moms. Emma's mom is holding glue and a cup of water.

"It looks fantastic, girls," Mrs Witte says approvingly.

"All right, let's mix this stuff until we get the perfect concoction. I checked, and Charlotte was right. Here you go, Emma," Mom says, handing her the glue, water, and an empty jar.

Once combined, Emma takes the paintbrush and starts stroking the mix over the entire collage to give it all a smooth matte finish. Gypsy wakes up from under the table as Emma accidentally nudges his head with her shoe. He gives Emma a disturbed look and slowly lifts his large, long-haired body and shuffles himself to the other side of the room.

"Sorry, Gypsy, didn't mean to be in your way. Wish you could see how many pictures you're in!" Emma tells him and takes a look at the almost finished project. One corner of her desk is still empty.

"Which pictures are you going to put there?" Mom asks.

"None, for now." Emma replies. "That space is for new memories. It was Charlotte's idea."

"Excellent!" Mom gives Charlotte a smile filled with appreciation.

"Mom, I know we're taking many things with us, and memories, but what about some of the things we always *do* together here, will we do them over there as well?"

"Like what, sweetie?"

"Like … *Sinterklaas*, Christmas, and Easter egg hunts … but also the things we do more often, like Pancake Wednesday." Emma looks at Mrs Witte, because Pancake Wednesday, at either Emma's or Charlotte's house, has become a tradition over the years.

"Of course we'll keep celebrating those things, Emma," Mom says, "even if we can't have Pancake Wednesday every week."

"And whenever you'll come visit, I promise we'll make pancakes," Mrs Witte assures her.

"Good deal!" Mom says, rubbing Emma's back.

"You know, just because you move away doesn't mean traditions need to end," Mrs Witte waves at the desk. "Remember, when your family went to our chalet in Gryon for the first time for a ski holiday when you were only four years old? And how you kept going back to that little hut even after you moved to Switzerland, and then when you moved back to Stolwijk?"

"You'll keep your traditions, Emma," Charlotte puts her arm around her friend, "but just like the white space on your desk, you'll need to make room for new traditions as well."

"I guess we'll end up with a lot of traditions," Emma says smiling.

That evening, Emma shows Dad her new desktop.

"Great!" he says. "I really love it, Emma, maybe I'll ask you to do one for me too," he adds with a wink.

"In case you're wondering, the empty space is to add new memories."

"That sounds like a very good idea." Dad sits down in a kitchen chair. "Hey Em, Mom told me on the phone you're a little worried about us forgetting our traditions once we move."

"Yeah, I guess I am," Emma admits, as she is still admiring her piece of art.

"Well, on the way home today I was thinking about our traditions. Do you remember my little tradition of picking up a chestnut for you – if I can find one – wherever I go on a business trip? I thought perhaps we should start a new tradition with this new move."

"Like what?" Emma asks.

"I'm not sure yet, but you know how we've had that one pear tree in the garden since the year you were born? Every time I look at it, I think of you, how much you've grown and all the memories we've created together over the years. And then, the other day, I was reading about a little girl called Ruth, who also moved around a lot when she was a young girl. And her father once told her, 'Ruth, wherever you go in life, unpack your bags – physically and mentally – and plant your trees'. So with this brand new garden we'll have, I thought maybe we could plant a tree together that we both really like and watch it grow for as long as we live there."

"I like that," Emma says, her face lighting up. "But then what if we move again?"

"We'll plant a new one there," Dad answers. "And then one day you can visit all of your trees, think of our memories together and see how much they have grown."

"Okay," Emma agrees.

"And maybe," Dad adds, "it will also remind you of how you have grown, and I don't mean in height, but as a person."

Emma hugs Dad. "I think I'd like that. A whole new tradition! Can we make it a chestnut tree?"

"Let's do that!" Dad laughs. "Who knows how many trees we'll plant!"

Emma thinks back to the conversation earlier that day and is beginning to understand how this move, how *any* move, can also mean the start of new traditions.

B IS ATTACHED WITH A SCARF TO A BELT LOOP IN EMMA'S jeans. Emma carefully climbs into the branches of her favorite willow tree, using the little pieces of wood nailed to the trunk by Dad a while back. B dangles along and sometimes feels a branch scratching his face as they are making their way up to the tree house. Emma has taken her painting materials and her mini iPod, which tells him she is ready for some alone time.

"I'm going to paint the view from here," she tells B, spreading out her paints and brushes on the wooden floor of the tree house.

"It's not for me, it's for Dad," Emma explains. B is unsure why his presence is required, but as soon as Emma uses him as a pillow to sit on, it becomes clear. Emma leans back against one of the thick tree branches that is holding up the floor, pulls her knees up and rests her sketchbook on them. B looks around and wonders how much she will miss this great spot, her little sanctuary where she loves being on her own or with friends.

From the corner of his eye, B sees Dad taking a picture of them. *I guess Emma is not the only one recording memories around here,* B thinks. Gypsy is sitting at Dad's feet, scouting his beloved big green yard for any visiting cats. B finds it rather endearing to watch Emma painting the view Dad loves so very much, while Dad is taking a picture of Emma in her favorite tree house. *They both want to capture a special place for the other.*

While listening to Emma's fears and anticipation, B has also been observing Daan and Sophia. He often thinks about what this move means to them. For Daan, it's obviously an improvement for his career and he must be looking forward to his new position. He seems much more preoccupied with everything that will change for him in the office, rather than how their lives will change at home. Recently, he's been walking around with his camera an awful lot though. Mostly he captures pictures of the house and the beautiful view of the sun setting over the farm fields. It's almost like Daan thinks they won't be moving back here any time soon, or at all. B wonders if Emma realizes that this move might mean she will never again live in the house where she was born.

As for Sophia, he once overheard her saying that the move back to the Netherlands after two years in Zurich felt like stepping into an old pair of shoes. Not the pair that are comfortable to slip into again, but the worn-out pair you are ready to toss away. B figures that Sophia is very excited about moving to a new place. Especially after the negative experiences during this past year, first the fire and then her mother passing away. She seems to long for a breath of fresh air and a place to open her own horizons.

Even though the family is moving from one place to another together, they are each experiencing the transition very differently. The move in itself has a separate meaning for each of them and the consequences of the move are so individual. Yet they will also one day remember them together as part of their family history.

"Does Dad prefer the sunset when it's all red or when it shows different shades of orange and pink?" Emma wonders aloud. B has a feeling Dad will like the sunset on Emma's painting regardless of what color it is.

8

Lost in Translation

"Emma, dinner's ready! Come down, please!"
Emma has just finished packing her weekend bag
when she hears Mom calling for her. Tomorrow,
after school, they are taking off to Luxembourg for
a long weekend. Emma even gets to skip school on
Monday so that they will be able to visit her new
school. Emma looks at the contents of her bag and
carefully tucks in her Moving Booklet before she
walks downstairs.

"So, Emma, what are you most excited about for
this weekend?" Dad pours her a glass of milk, her
favorite dinner drink. Dad always asks her what she
is most or least excited about, or what the best or
worst part of her day or vacation was. She usually

87

has a hard time pinpointing things. Especially now, with so many thoughts running through her head.

"I don't know. I guess visiting the new school."

"Well, that *is* exciting," Mom says, filling up Emma's plate with spaghetti and sauce, a meal which tells her Mom is a little busy right now.

"What about seeing the new house? Are you looking forward to that?" Dad asks, raising his glass in the air briefly to 'cheers' Mom and her as he always does right before dinner.

"Not so much," Emma says, "I mean, it's not even finished yet, right?"

"No, but I bet it'll be good to get an idea of where we'll be living soon," Mom says, giving Emma a quick nod as a cue that she can start eating now they're all served up.

"Anything you're worried about?" Dad asks.

"Hmmm, I guess I already speak much better English now, so that's a little less of a worry this time." Emma digs her fork into the long strings of pasta and starts twirling them around it.

"Were you very worried about it when we moved to Zurich?" Mom asks.

"You don't remember the bathroom incident?" Emma asks with a tone of astonishment.

"Ah, yes, I do," Mom says, with a hint of guilt on her face.

"What incident? I don't remember." Dad looks at Emma and Mom.

"Emma had gotten a little bit 'lost and found in translation' on her first day of school there," Mom begins to explain.

Emma remembers her first day at the American School of Zurich very clearly. She had immediately liked her teacher, Mrs Love, who was as sweet as her name sounded. She was very young, had a big mane of brown hair, and was very soft-spoken.

Emma had looked around the beautifully decorated classroom wondering who her new friends would be. There were so many children who looked different from her. In the Netherlands they had all looked a lot like each other. In this new class, there had been boys and girls with different skin colors and some had very, very dark hair and eyes. However, they had all been smiling at her and this had made her feel really welcome.

There was a slight problem though; she had not known how to communicate with them. Mom had assured her she would learn English in no time. Unfortunately, she quickly found out there was one pressing English phrase she wished she had learned before that first day of school.

"I really, really had to go pee, but I didn't know how to ask Mrs Love in English where the bathroom was," Emma continues to explain to Dad. "So I slipped out of the classroom without telling her and began to look for the toilets. I think I toured the entire school three times on my own before I finally found a door with a toilet sign on it!"

"Wasn't Mrs Love worried about where you'd gone?" Dad asks.

"She was! Once I was done, I was about to open the door to try find my way back, and I almost bumped right into Mrs Love. I thought I'd be in trouble, but she just smiled at me, grabbed my hand and walked me back. She then knocked on the door of the classroom next to ours and said something to the teacher there. He called for one of the students to come over, and she turned to me and started speaking in Dutch! It was such a relief!"

"Smart teacher," Dad laughs. "What did the girl say?"

"That I needed to ask the teacher for permission to go to the bathroom. I told her I didn't know how to say that. So she taught me how to say it and showed me the bathroom that was right next to her classroom!" Emma can laugh about it all now.

"So that was your first English lesson?" Dad serves himself some more spaghetti and sauce.

"Yup!" Emma wonders how many school stories he misses out on because he is so busy working, but she is always happy when he is eager to listen.

"Well, you're right. This time you won't need to worry about the language barrier. Your English is already quite good and it will only get better," Dad says encouragingly.

"I know, I just hope there will be some nice kids there. I really like my friends here," Emma says. Suddenly, the sound of Skype ringing interrupts the conversation.

Mom takes a peek at her laptop sitting on the kitchen counter. "It's Emilie, Emma."

"Can I go talk to her, please?" Emma pleads, hoping to be excused from dinner. Even though her friend moved to another town a couple of years ago, they still talk every few weeks. Last summer, Emilie also came along with them on a holiday to Spain.

"If you finish up that last bite," Mom says.

"Thanks." Emma sucks down her last spaghetti strands.

Mom presses the little green Skype camera button and brings the laptop computer to the table.

"Hi, Emilie! I just finished dinner," Emma says. "Let me walk up to my room."

"Hi, Emma! Hi, Mr and Mrs V!" Emilie waves at Emma's parents, who wave back as Emma trails off to her room with Emilie on the screen.

"So, how are you doing?" B hears Emilie ask, when Emma reaches her room.

"Good. A little nervous about our trip to Luxembourg this weekend." Emma makes herself comfortable on her little white couch.

"Trust me, it does make a difference meeting some of your new classmates before actually moving," Emilie says.

"I know, and I'm excited, but I can't help feeling a little sad. Now that we're going to be saying hello, it also means we're definitely going to be saying goodbye," Emma confesses.

"I know how difficult it is to get used to a new school and new friends. But you know there'll be some cool boys and girls there." B listens to Emilie's consoling words.

"Yeah, I know. It's weird to think there are people out there who I haven't met yet, but some of them will probably become as important to me as my friends now," Emma replies.

"Exactly! I bet a visit like this would be impossible if you were moving much further away," Emilie says. "Don't worry, you'll have fun."

And you can always Skype your friends from here, too, B wants to add. He thinks back to his friends in the shop. There was always a slight pain in his heart every time one of these friends was taken off the shelf forever. Part of it was jealousy. *Why didn't they pick me?* Mostly it was the loss of a friendship that hurt him. Friendships were like ships moving from shore to shore, never staying anchored in one port for a very long time.

When he finally left, B was very sad to leave his friends behind. He not only understands Emma's pain, he's seen it before. B remembers how upset Emma had been when she left behind her friends in Zurich three years ago. Using him as a thick handkerchief, she had cried so much one evening B had thought he was going to stay wet forever.

The first few weeks back in the Netherlands had not been the easiest for Emma either. She would complain to B that the other kids had already known each other for so long. She came into a class of kids who had been together since preschool. They were not used to the comings and goings of classmates like the children in international schools. However, after several weeks, she stopped talking to B and he knew she had started to make new friends.

"I kind of wish I had a brother or sister to share all this with," B hears Emma say to Emilie.

"Be careful what you wish for! My younger sisters can be real pests!" Emilie laughs.

B had heard Emma beg for a little brother or sister on so many occasions. Mom would reply, with sadness wrapped up in hopefulness, that they wish they could give her one. Somehow that still hasn't happened. Instead, her friends and cousins are always welcome to come over for play dates or sleepovers, and sometimes even on vacations. Although it would never entirely replace having a sibling, Emma never seemed to be truly lonely or lacking attention.

"Are you allowed to have a Facebook page yet?" Emilie asks.

"No, Mom and Dad won't let me. They say I'm still too young. Are you?" Emma asks with envy.

"No, but if you ask your mom to befriend your friends' moms then you can at least see what they're up to. That's what we did." Emilie is definitely a good person to talk to about moving. B can tell she is cheering Emma up.

"So do you think you can come over for a weekend before the summer vacation?" Emma asks Emilie.

"Yes! I was calling about that, too. When is a good weekend?"

B stops listening as the girls make plans. He is definitely a little jealous of all the ways they have of keeping in touch and spending time together. In his world, a friend apart just means a friend in the heart.

9

A New Country

"Are we there yet?" Emma asks her parents, fully aware how annoying they find that question. The drive from Stolwijk to Luxembourg was taking longer than Emma had hoped.

"Not long now, sweetie, we just drove into Luxembourg, so another half hour before we reach the hotel," Mom replies from the front.

"Are we going to see the new house today?" Emma asks.

"No, tomorrow. This afternoon we'll see a little bit of the town and go to bed early. We have two very busy days ahead of us," Dad answers.

Finally, after five hours of driving, Emma and her parents check into a big hotel on a hill. It is the tallest building for miles and sticks out like a skinny pencil.

"Is this really where we're going to live for the first few months?" Emma asks Mom, unsure if she loves or hates the idea of living in a hotel for that long.

"The real estate agent said we might be able to move into our new house a bit earlier than we thought, but this is what we'll have to call home for a few weeks after we move."

Emma can tell by the excited tone in Mom's voice that she's thrilled about not doing any cleaning, laundry or cooking for a while.

The lobby has a big fountain in the middle and cool glass elevators that allow you to watch the ground become smaller and smaller as you rise up.

Mom and Dad talk to the receptionist and get the keycard for their room. Emma is holding Gypsy on his leash. He starts to sniff around and gently pulls Emma along. *Smart dog,* she thinks, and pats his back as he guides her towards the restaurant. Emma pokes her head into the main entrance and catches a whiff of what the diners are eating. *Yum, french fries! Maybe this whole living in a hotel thing won't be such a hassle after all,* she thinks.

Right before breakfast the following morning, Emma and Dad take the glass elevator all the way down to the hotel spa. Emma has never been in a spa.

"Wow, croissants!" Emma exclaims as they walk into an area lined with deck chairs right next to the indoor pool.

"Those are for after, Emma," Dad says in a semi-stern voice, "First, we swim some laps to earn them!"

Emma longingly looks at the croissants but dives into the water and swims twenty laps before rewarding herself with one. She could get used to this.

Dad seems to be reading her mind. "Enjoy it while it lasts Emma, but don't get too used to this! Once we move into the house there won't be a pool."

"I know, Dad, but it makes me like the idea of living in a hotel more than I thought."

"So, it won't be so bad to come here for a while?"

"I guess not too bad," Emma replies, trying to conceal a smile.

"You know, Em," Dad says, getting up from the chair and flinging his towel over his shoulder, "sometimes you have to throw all expectations out the window, because *toujours l'inattendu arrive.*"

Emma doesn't need another French lesson to understand that phrase Dad would always use ... *the unexpected always shows up.* She has to admit, mostly to herself, that living in a gorgeous hotel for a few weeks is certainly nothing worth complaining about.

WHILE EMMA AND DAD ARE TAKING A SWIM, B IS SITTING upstairs in the hotel room.

He cannot help but think of the numerous hotel rooms he has seen, thanks to Emma. He should say, thanks to Sophia. One of the perks of her job as a flight attendant is that, for a fraction of the usual ticket price, she can take Daan and Emma with her on trips while working.

At least once a year they can go to some far-off place. B always enjoys the anticipation of whether there will be spaces left on the plane for their standby seats, but so far they have always been lucky. Sometimes he feels like Emma has no idea how privileged she is to have seen so much of the world so young.

He couldn't complain either. B had traveled to four continents, seen animals most people (or teddy bears) only get to see in a zoo, experienced the hustle and bustle of cosmopolitan cities, and admired many a beautiful foreign countryside. By far, his favorite part of traveling was listening to all the different languages.

Of course B couldn't speak any language, but he could still listen and get a sense of what people were trying to communicate. That's why it never bothered him when Emma switched languages on him.

One night, when they had just moved back to Stolwijk after Zurich, B had heard Emma yell at Sophia and Daan that she was able to speak three languages, but wasn't able to express herself fluently in any of them.

"Sometimes, I can't remember a word in Dutch and when I say it in English, others look at me as if I'm trying to impress them," Emma complained, "when all I'm trying to do is use the word that seems to suit the situation."

B understands that it isn't easy trying to learn a new language. While Daan and Sophia had struggled to learn German, let alone Swiss German, it seemed as if Emma had an advantage being so much younger – it seemed easier for her to learn the new language than it did for her parents. When she was playing with her Swiss German neighbor, he had heard her picking up the language as she went along. And then at the American School of Zurich, she was immersed into the English language and took German lessons. B always thought her knowledge of three languages blended into one. It was her own language and made perfect sense to her. And to him.

"And some words are impossible to translate into any other language," Emma had continued. "Like *gezellig*. There's no word for that. It's not exactly 'cozy' and it's not *gemütlich* either," Emma had said, translating a Dutch word into the two other languages she knew.

B hopes Daan and Sophia will continue to speak to Emma in Dutch, because it's so important for her to stay connected with her mother tongue and Dutch culture. Knowing her own language well will also help her become fluent in other languages.

Emma did not yet understand the advantages of being exposed to lots of languages, especially while she was so young. It would be one of the many things she'd be thankful for one day, of that B was sure.

B watches Emma and Dad walk back in the door, both wearing hotel bathrobes. Emma is smiling and has croissant crumbs sticking to her chin as she walks towards the bathroom to take a shower. She hops in, and he hears her yell out, "Wow, Mom, Dad, did you see all the soaps and shampoos they give us? It's like a little shop in here!"

Perhaps the positives of this move are beginning to outweigh the negatives for Emma, B thinks, a little relieved.

10

A New House

THAT AFTERNOON, EMMA AND HER PARENTS VISIT THE new house. Gypsy is panting in the back of the car and Emma feels a big blob of slobber hit her shoulder. Usually she would get annoyed by Gypsy's smelly drools, but now she's just happy he is coming with them. Poor Gypsy won't have a yard to play in the first few weeks at the hotel. Emma promised her parents she would take him for lots of walks, but she really hopes this new house will have plenty of space for him to run outside.

Emma looks out of the car window and reads the sign announcing her new hometown. It starts with the same two letters as their town in the Netherlands. Stolwijk and Steinsel. The only thing these two places have in common is St, because they couldn't look any more different. Stolwijk is a small farming town and their little cottage – that once upon a time used to be an old farm barn – is located at the end of a very flat road, surrounded by little canals. This brand new house in Steinsel is built in the middle of a steep hill, in a very modern looking neighborhood.

"All right then, here we are," Dad says happily as they pull into the driveway. The house isn't close to being finished yet and is still missing its doors and windows. Emma immediately doesn't like it and already misses the cozy feel of their little cottage with its new, golden thatch roof.

"Come on, Emma, let's go have a look around," Mom says as she steps out of the car.

The house looks almost eerily deserted in its construction state on this quiet Sunday afternoon. Emma can see Mom trying to think of what the house will look like once it is finished. Emma is not sure she can yet, and she is not sure she cares either. However, she has to admit that she is a little curious about what her room will look like. Reluctantly, Emma steps out of the car.

Mom and Dad walk her through the whole house, opening their arms wide and spinning round in every room. She wonders whether they have enough stuff to fill up the whole place. It's huge! As they walk up the staircase, she looks all the way back down towards the basement. In Stolwijk they didn't even have a basement. *What do people need one for anyway?* She lets her hand brush the wall. *Well, hello new house.* It dawns on her that this house has no history yet, that these walls have seen and heard nothing, and that they are as new to her as she is new to them.

"And this will be your room. What do you think?" Mom asks her as they stand in a room about three times the size of her old one.

"It's massive," Emma says with a slightly embarrassed smile, walking towards the window overlooking the big garden.

"Not what you expected, Emma?" Dad winks at her.

"You'll also get your own bathroom. How about that?" Mom says, crossing the hallway into a bathroom that doesn't look much smaller than the one she shares with her parents right now.

Emma can't believe how much space there is. She follows her parents into their new room, with a walk-in closet and en suite bathroom, just like the one they have in the hotel right now.

"You guys even get your own balcony!" Emma exclaims, walking onto the balcony that overlooks the street. She leans over the railing, moving her head from left to right to left. Suddenly, from the corner of her eye, she sees three girls around her own age playing in the front garden a couple of houses away. They spot her as well and give a friendly wave.

Emma waves back and then turns to look at Mom who is giving her a reassuring wink.

"So what do you think, Emma?" Dad asks, inspecting the balcony rail.

"It's nice," Emma starts off, "but it's not ..."

"Not like home?" Mom asks while leaning over the railing.

"Uh-huh. It's nothing like home."

"You just wait and see, kiddo, once all our own furniture and stuff have found a spot of their own, it will feel like home in no time," Mom assures her. "And look at this view! You always wanted to live on a street with other children to play with. It looks like there are plenty," she says, motioning to the girls down the street.

"I know," Emma nods. She walks back to 'her' room and starts imagining where she is going to put her bed, her desk, her closet, and her couch.

As she looks at the bare concrete floor, she hears Mom walking in.

"What color carpet would you like, Emma? You get to choose," Mom says, as if she is reading Emma's mind.

"Really? *Any* color?"

"Your pick."

"Pink." Emma immediately replies, looking at Mom casting a disapproving look right away. "Please," she adds.

"Absolutely sure?" Mom clearly hopes that Emma will change her mind.

"For sure, sure."

"All right, pink it is then, but I don't think I'll ask your advice about the living room carpet," Mom says jokingly.

Back outside, they step onto the big terrace, bordering a spacious yard. Dad is throwing a stick out towards the big mud patch that will hopefully be a beautiful green lawn someday. Gypsy is happily running after it.

"Emma, can you already think of a place to plant our tree?" Dad asks.

"What about right there, where Gypsy's standing now?" Emma replies, watching the dog grab hold of the stick. He firmly shakes it from left to right a few times. At least one of them is already enjoying their new place.

Emma and her parents decide to have some lunch in Luxembourg City. Afterwards, they wander through the main streets, getting a feel of the quaint and charming town. Dad shows them where his new office will be, just around the corner from the main square. After some sightseeing, they drive back to the hotel.

"All right, ladies, I'll take Gypsy for a long walk before we have dinner," Dad says, dropping Mom and Emma off at the hotel door.

"Are we going to eat down at the restaurant again tonight?" Emma asks hopefully.

"We will, but once we're living here we'll use the little kitchenette and do some of our own cooking. Don't get too used to those french fries," Mom answers, laughing.

"I'm sure the novelty of the hotel will wear off soon enough," Dad reassures Mom. "By the end of our stay here, we'll be more than eager to move into the new house. Even our french fry-loving daughter!"

"Hmmm," Emma replies. But her mind has already wandered off to her new room.

When Emma and her parents leave to visit the new house, B looks around the room from his unfamiliar bed. He doesn't really like this hotel room at all. The bed is too big and he misses the comfort of familiar sights around him. *Perhaps I'm not as adventurous as I used to be,* he thinks.

When the door opens, B waits for the sound of familiar voices. Emma must have forgotten something. Instead he hears someone humming a soft song. B is not used to having strangers coming into his space unless Emma or Sophia accompanies them. He cannot see anyone, as Emma has left the sheets in disarray this morning. The corner of the duvet has been pulled right over his head. The sound of the person shuffling from one corner of the room to another makes him nervous.

Footsteps are coming closer to the bed and he is suddenly reminded of that helpless feeling on the night of the fire. He feels his body being flung into the air. Momentarily he senses a wonderful feeling of freedom and lightness, then the sheets close in on his body as they are pressed together by two hands. Finally, he is tossed into what feels like a big sack of some sort.

"One bed done, two to go," a female voice mutters to herself. Uh-oh! B is on the move now and he can hear the squeak of tiny wheels as he is pushed this way and that before stopping for a while. Then another pile of sheets lands on his head. It squashes him down further and he begins to panic.

Again the cart is moving, and for a moment B thinks the lady may have noticed her mistake when he feels two arms scoop him up, buried inside the sheets. But instead of being rescued by her, he feels her hands shoving the big bundle around him into some sort of hole. Oh, no! He can feel himself falling down and down, as if he is were on a slide at the playground. Once more, B thinks back to the fire and fears the worst. This fall takes much longer, and for some reason it is completely dark around him. He lands softly, not in the muddy garden, but in a pile of slightly smelly sheets.

It's not until hours later that B overhears what happened that morning.

"Dad, you are never going to guess where B ended up today!" Emma blurts out as Daan and Gypsy return from their afternoon walk.

"Tell me," Dad says.

"When I was sitting on my bed, filling in my Moving Booklet, I was looking for B and couldn't find him in my bed. Mom and I looked everywhere, but he was nowhere to be found."

"Needless to say, Emma was getting a little upset," Mom adds putting her index finger and thumb together to indicate 'a little'. Sophia seems to think that Emma's bravado right now doesn't reflect her intense sadness of earlier. B agrees.

"Right. So we went down to the reception area and there was this really sweet receptionist, Helga, who told us that she once lost her koala bear when she was my age, so she totally understood. We explained that we thought housekeeping might have dropped him into the laundry. So Helga called down to the laundry and they let us go have a look down there."

"It certainly is impressive how many washing machines and dryers a hotel like this has," B hears Sophia say.

"Wait, Mom is not ever allowed to wash B at home and now he ended up in an industrial sized washing machine?" Dad asks incredulously.

"I know! I was so scared we were never going to find him, because those machines are huge and there was so *much* laundry down there!"

Mom adds, "One of the ladies made it quite clear to us that if we wanted to find him, we had to dig through all the piles ourselves. So we did."

"How long did it take you to find him?" Dad asks.

"How do you know we found him?" Emma responds with a look of disappointment in her eyes, wanting to keep the suspense going for a bit longer.

"Well, sweetheart, if you hadn't you'd be absolutely devastated and in tears right now."

B looks at Emma, waiting for her reaction. She grins and says, "I guess you're right, but we did find him! It was amazing, Mom pulled him straight out of one of the washing machines, all wet and soggy!"

B certainly isn't too impressed with the 'bath' he received and was absolutely horrified by the dryer experience after that. Sophia had asked the laundry ladies if he could be tossed in one of the dryers just for five minutes to remedy his soaked state. It had, without question, been the most terrifying experience of his life. That monster had tossed him around like a squash ball being hit from wall to wall.

B isn't sure how to forgive Emma for this one, but he eventually will. He knows it wasn't entirely her fault, but he sure wishes she'd be a little more careful at times.

11

A New School

EARLY THE NEXT MORNING, MOM AND EMMA DROP Dad off at his new office and continue on to Emma's new school. As they drive up and down plenty of steep hills, Emma realizes that unless there is some kind of secret tunnel cutting through these hills, there is no way she will ever be able to bike to school. To avoid thinking about this for too long, she takes out the Moving Booklet from her bag and opens it up to the 'My New School' page. First item to fill in: Three things to look forward to.

"All right, I'd better find out about at least three things," Emma mumbles to herself.

"Are you ready to go in?" Mom asks, pulling into the parking lot of her future school. It is a gorgeous looking building with big wide windows and white brick. It doesn't look anything like Emma's school in Gouda. Mom begins to tell her it is a historic building, but the only words she picks up is 'old convent'. She's too busy checking it all out.

"Do you know where we're going?" Emma asks Mom as they walk towards the front entrance.

"To the principal's office. He emailed to say he would give us a tour of the school this morning," Mom replies, opening the door for her. Inside, there is a sign pointing to the office.

The hallway is narrow, and Emma peeks through the windows on both sides of the corridor until they are forced to turn sharp right. There is a sign saying *Principal Preston Evans*. The door is open and a friendly looking lady is sitting behind a desk.

"Good morning, you must be Emma," she says as she gets up to walk around her desk. She shakes Emma's hand and then introduces herself to Mom. "Hi, I'm Sue, Principal Evans' secretary," she says, "I'll let him know you're here."

"Good morning," a loud booming voice echoes through the waiting area. A man who looks more like Father Christmas than a stern principal walks out of his office. "Emma, welcome to the Inter-Community School of Luxembourg," he says with a twinkle in his eye and shakes her hand.

Emma quickly loses her sense of orientation as Principal Evans takes them through the maze of corridors in this sprawling building. Listening to him explain how the school works, she realizes she is looking forward to speaking English again.

"So, Emma, you'll be coming into fifth grade next year, right?" Principal Evans asks her as they stand in front of the school cafeteria. The morning recess bell rings and kids pour into the cafeteria from all sides.

"Yes, sir," she answers.

"Well, let me introduce you to some of the students who will be in your class," he says, opening the door to the cafeteria for her. "Just wait here a moment, please," he says to Mom.

Emma looks at Mom and raises her eyebrows a little as if to question whether it's okay. After Mom gives her an encouraging look she follows Principal Evans to one of the tables.

"Good morning ladies and gentlemen, this is Emma. She'll be coming to this school after the summer vacation and will be in your class. I would appreciate it if you would give her a warm welcome and answer any questions she may have about the school. And don't just tell her about your mean, cranky principal," he adds with a big wink, tapping the table with his knuckles and pulling out a chair for Emma with his other hand.

The students at the table chuckle and some of them roll their eyes, in an amused way.

"Hi, I'm Carolyn," a girl with big brown hair and a bright orange sweater offers. "And this is Aneta, Keiko, Lynda, Drew, Geoff, Karen and Elias," pointing to each of the other students.

"Where are you from?" Keiko asks.

"The Netherlands," Emma hesitates, wishing the answer would end there, "but I also lived in Switzerland for a few years. What about all of you?"

"Ha! Are you really ready to listen to all the answers?" a boy with a heavy accent asks her with a big grin. Emma tries to remember his name but has already forgotten. She looks at him and feels her cheeks getting a little flushed. He's very cute and she immediately loves the fact he doesn't seem to be ashamed of his accent.

"I'm from the States, but we've lived here for five years already," Carolyn answers.

"I'm half Polish and half American, and we're moving to Kenya in January," Aneta, a tall, blond girl says.

"I'm from Japan," Keiko, a girl with a cute black bob cut says, "but we only arrived here a month ago. We're planning stay here for at least two years."

"I'm from Australia," Lynda says, "but my mom is from Luxembourg and we're staying here for good now."

A boy with a baseball cap says, "I'm originally from the States, but we lived in Hong Kong for five years before moving here. And before that we lived in

Tanzania for two years. We've lived in Luxembourg for three years now. Oh, and my name is Drew."

His neighbor coyly says, "I'm Geoff and I'm from England, but I've lived here forever."

Next, a tall girl with a friendly expression says, "Hi, I'm Karen and I'm from Sweden."

Finally, they've come full circle and the cute boy says, "Me too, Karen and I are twins. We came this year from Sweden, but we lived in Thailand and in Nepal when we were really little. Oh, and my name is Elias."

"Wow," Emma says, "That's a lot of different countries." She had forgotten how very mixed a class could be. Everyone here is from different places and they have all lived in Luxembourg for different amounts of time. In her class in Gouda, pretty much everyone had always lived in the same town!

"Yes, we all find it difficult to answer the question 'Where are you from?' in one sentence, let alone one word," Drew says.

"People quickly lose interest in your story if you make it too long," Aneta adds. "My mom says you should be able to give someone all the information they need to know within ten seconds. If they're truly interested in the rest of your story, they'll ask. If not, why waste more time explaining yourself?"

Good point, Emma thinks to herself. She is feeling at home already.

"I usually tell them that I'm from everywhere ..." Elias starts.

"... and nowhere!" Karen finishes her brother's sentence.

"But right now, home is here," Elias adds.

So home is somewhere between here and everywhere, Emma thinks to herself. She smiles back at Elias and really hopes she isn't blushing as much as she feels she is.

When they leave the school building, Mom puts her arm around her.

"So, do you think you might like this school?"

"I have a feeling I might just fit in fine here," Emma replies confidently, as a grin from ear to ear appears on her face.

B ALWAYS ENJOYS IT WHEN EMMA'S FRIENDS ARE AT THE house for a sleepover. This time it's a full house. Emma has invited Mimi, Charlotte and Emilie over, all at the same time. Charlotte and Emilie know each other from preschool and Mimi and Emilie seem to get along fine too.

Apparently, the four girls have spent the afternoon playing with a little dinghy boat in the small canals around Emma's house. After showers and dinner, they make themselves comfortable in the big guest room. When Emma comes to get her duvet and pillow from her room, without a moment of hesitation, she picks B up and tucks him under her arm. Lucky for him, because he loves listening in on the girls' conversations.

"So when will you be able to move all your stuff?" Mimi asks.

"Not until the house is finished completely, so in a few months time," Emma answers.

"What will happen to all your furniture and things in the mean time?" Charlotte questions.

"We'll need to put it in storage. Dad says it will feel like my birthday once I get to unpack everything again."

"I bet you're not leaving B in storage though?" Emilie gently pats Emma's bear, she has grown attached to him over the years as well.

"No way! But I'll have to be careful he won't be thrown in with the laundry again."

"Is he smelling more like B again yet?" Mimi asks.

"He's starting to. It's funny because the morning before B was lost in the laundry, I smelled him when I was still lying in bed. His smell immediately reminded me of home, but then I opened my eyes and realized we were in a hotel room in Luxembourg."

B is wondering what he smells like. He knows what Emma, Sophia, Daan, and even the big hairy dog smell like to him, but he has no idea what he smells like to others. According to Emma, he smells like 'home'. But what if someone else smells him? Surely their nose will not be greeted by an overwhelming whiff of familiarity.

"Isn't it amazing how smells can bring back memories?" Emilie responds. "Whenever I drive past farm fields and smell fresh manure, it reminds me of Stolwijk."

The other girls giggle at Emilie's comment about manure.

"I have it when we eat cheese fondue," Charlotte adds. "It's a wave of cheese odor that makes me feel like we're up in our chalet in Switzerland."

"I wonder if your sense of smell helps you remember people and places," Emma wonders out loud. "Because if you aren't reminded of them by smells then perhaps those memories slowly fade away."

B hopes that his smell can help her hold on to certain memories of home. *But,* he wonders, *will the smell of home change a little as the years go by and home changes location?*

"So, Emma, did you ask your parents about sailing camp?" Mimi asks.

"Yes! We talked about it last night and I'm allowed to go!" Emma says.

"Oh, that's so cool," Charlotte chimes in, and then turns to Emilie. "You should come, too!"

"I'm already going to a horse back riding camp for a week," Emilie says, "so I don't think I'll be allowed to go to another camp, but thanks for asking."

"Will you come to Emma's going away party though?" Mimi asks. Mimi and Charlotte have taken it upon themselves to organize a party for Emma before she leaves.

"Of course! Wouldn't miss it for the world," Emilie answers.

B thinks how nice it is that Emma's friends are eager to give her a good send-off, as well keeping her included in their activities for as long as possible.

12

Saying Goodbye
and Saying Hello

Emma holds the doorknob in her hand and turns around one more time to face her bare and empty room. It doesn't even look like her bedroom anymore.

"Bye," she whispers and blows the walls a kiss before closing the door for the last time. Walking down the stairs, Emma thinks back to last night. She still feels tired, but she is so grateful to her friends for organizing such a great going away party. She gives the pillow that's tucked under her arm a firm squeeze as if to make sure it's really there.

'This is to remember us by, every evening, Emma. Even when your mind is filled with thoughts of your new home, and school, and friends, we hope you will always keep us in your heart and remember us forever,' the card had read. The whole pillowcase was decorated with all her classmates' signatures, flowers, hearts, smiley faces, thoughts of encouragement and words to let her know she was being missed already.

Mimi had written, 'See you at sailing camp in two weeks, I can't wait!' Knowing she would still spend an entire week with her friends during the summer made saying goodbye a little easier.

As promised, Emilie had come over especially too. She had given Emma a beautiful little wooden box. 'Put something smelly in here that reminds you of Stolwijk,' Emilie had written on a note, 'but probably not cow manure!' Leave it up to Emilie to give her something to help her laugh. Emma had put some pebbles from the garden into it and some fresh lavender. After the fire, Mom had put fresh lavender sachets *everywhere* to get rid of the awful ashtray smell. As a result, Emma had begun to associate its sweet scent with their restored cottage.

I'm not really saying goodbye to any of my friends here forever, Emma thought to herself as she stepped into the car, *I'm just saying goodbye to this part of my life. It doesn't mean my true friends can't be part of my new one.*

As Dad starts the engine, Emma places the pillow on her lap. Slowly they start to drive away. Emma first turns her head and then her whole body around to sit on her knees facing backwards. In one hand she is clutching B, and with the other she starts to wave goodbye to their beautiful, cozy cottage. She feels Mom turning around. She is probably biting her tongue, wanting to tell her to put her seatbelt on. Finally, as they turn out of their lane, Emma turns forward again, clicks her seatbelt in and props the pillow underneath her head. Gypsy gently nudges her hair as if to say that he is sorry too. She places B by the side of her head between the window and her cheek. Cocooned in her seat, she soon falls into a deep sleep.

When she wakes up, they are about to cross the border into Luxembourg.

"Almost there, sweetie." Mom turns around and gives her hand a reassuring squeeze. Emma can't believe she slept for almost five hours. She looks out of her window and recognizes some of the landscape from their visit a couple of months ago.

"Hey, look! There's a sign for the town where my school is," Emma points out to her parents.

"Are you looking forward to going?" Dad asks.

"Hmmm," Emma says trying not to sound too excited, "I guess. It definitely helps knowing where I'll be going."

"Are you still okay about spending some weeks in the hotel before moving into the house?" Mom asks.

"Absolutely," Emma says, as she thinks about the

beautiful hotel swimming pool and restaurant french fries. "Not sure B is though," she adds smiling.

"No more washing machines for him," Mom says. "Maybe we should agree to put him on the nightstand every morning to avoid any confusion."

"That's a good idea," Emma agrees as she gives B a squeeze.

Emma looks at B. *I won't lose you again. I promise.*

Here he is, back in the hotel bed, firmly tucked underneath Emma's head. While she rereads her latest entry in her Moving Booklet, B broods on how the pressure of her head on him every night is not doing much for his appearance.

Despite Sophia's well-intended patches, the seams around his paws keep loosening. One of his orange eyes is not fastened as firmly to his head anymore and the beige fur on his body is starting to wear down. He is looking less and less like a bear.

Compared to Emma, he's outwardly aging a lot faster. Inwardly, Emma is going through more changes. She isn't a little girl anymore, which means that, more frequently than before, he sees a side of her she isn't always willing to share with her parents or friends.

When she was younger, little tantrums would quickly turn to sadness and she would cry loudly for B. Once she could hold him closely to her cheek, she'd stick her thumb in her mouth and calm down within seconds.

These days Emma seems to control her emotions a little better in front of other people, but whenever she feels sad or upset she still grabs B and holds him close to her. Sometimes she still sucks her thumb, although since the dentist warned her she might have to wear a retainer to get rid of her overbite, she tries not to.

Tonight she is holding him close to her and he feels a few tears. Tomorrow is her first day at the Inter-Community School of Luxembourg, and B knows how anxious she is.

"I just want to go home. I just want to go home," she whispers.

Home as in the Netherlands? Home as in their old house? Home as in her old friends? Home as in a place she wasn't sure where it was? B wonders. *Or do you simply mean being home, belonging, like we talked about before?*

B is afraid Emma will start putting certain expectations on *home*. That she will always think she'll find comfort 'back home', when in truth, life happens to all of us and nothing ever really stays completely the same. And when you do go 'back home', it never is the exact same place you left behind. In the same way your new experiences will have shaped and slightly changed you.

B hears Sophia coming into the room.

"Time to turn the lights off, young lady. You have a big day ahead of you tomorrow."

Emma puts her book down and turns to the side of the bed where Mom is sitting. She readjusts B again underneath her head.

"Mom, what if we find out we're moving again in a few months?"

"I certainly hope not, but why do you ask?"

"Sometimes I wonder if it's worth all the effort ... I mean ... what if I have to say goodbye to my new classmates in a few months time? Then what's the point of becoming friends with them?"

"You can't live life according to 'what ifs'. If you spend all your time worrying about the 'what ifs', you'll never enjoy the 'here and nows'. Every day is worth making the best of. Today we're here, and all that matters is how you'll make today worth it. Sure, we might move again, but we'll cross that bridge when we get there."

"You're right, but knowing we might move again, it makes me feel like we're on a train, and that this is just a stop before the next stop and the stop after that. When do we reach our destination and get out of the train forever and unpack and ... settle down?"

"Okay. Think about it like this, Emma. You are on a train, but you're not getting off to walk up and down the platform at every stop. You get to explore all that's out there. At each place, you get to unpack, settle down, plant some seeds, and grow some roots. And when you move on, you take some of those roots and memories with you to the next place."

"Why can't the train just stop once and for all in one place?" Emma asks. Meanwhile B is starting to wonder if Emma really doesn't understand the positive twist Mom has given to her own metaphor of the train, or if she doesn't want to.

"Because life is like a train. It doesn't have one single destination. Life keeps moving along. Sometimes it might take you back to a place you were before, but either that spot will be a little different or you will look at it with different eyes because of all the other places *you've* seen."

"Hmmm," Emma grabs B from underneath her head, turns to her side and squeezes him towards her.

"Let's try to get some sleep now, all right?"

"Okay. Good night, Mom."

B feels Sophia's hand squeeze him as she kisses Emma's cheek.

"Good night, Emma, sleep well."

Just like every night, B listens to Emma's breathing slowly quiet down until she is in a deep slumber, off to her world of dreams. Somehow he has a feeling that there will be a train involved.

13

Things Change

"Are you ready?" Dad calls up from the bottom of the stairs.

"Coming!" Emma yells back. She is finishing up writing a sentence in her diary. She looks back at the date. October 21. She has lived in Luxembourg for a little over two months and they finally moved into the new house two weeks ago. Dad is waiting for her to go pick up Leila, Emma's older cousin, from the airport.

"What was taking you so long?" Dad asks as they get into the car. The *new* car. Emma hates it. She finds it pretentious and ridiculously big for their small family of three. The highly impractical sedan doesn't even have the proper space for a dog, so Gypsy and Emma share the backseat. She much prefers the older and smaller hatchback they brought from Stolwijk, but according to Dad he also needs a car that is 'suitable' for his job.

"Nothing," Emma replies as she realizes this is becoming her standard answer. She reconsiders and says, "I was writing in my diary."

"Okay," Dad says with a patient smile, yet not asking further about her diary entry. Emma notices he doesn't want to pry, but he's happy she is opening up a little to him.

"So, are you excited about showing Leila around your new home?" he carefully asks.

"Yeah, I guess," Emma replies. She knows she has been a bit distant with Dad, but sometimes it seems more difficult to confide in him than Mom these days. She decides she needs to try a little harder and give him a chance.

"You know, I feel like I'm fitting pretty well into this new life, it's just that ... I don't know," she continues.

"It's just what?" Dad asks in an encouraging voice.

"I guess I'm not sure my old life fits into my new life," Emma says.

"What do you mean? Will Leila's visit not fit into your life here?"

"No, it's fine she's coming to visit, but I'm scared she won't really understand my new life here. When I spoke to her on the phone, she made comments about us living in a hotel. Like we're being snooty on purpose or something."

"Well, in her eyes it is a little strange to be living in a hotel I guess, but you shouldn't worry too much about what she thinks. You do know that, right?" Dad asks.

"I know." Emma sighs. It reminds her of when she returned to the Netherlands and everyone thought she was so spoiled. Now that she'd left, people still only see the 'grass is greener'-part and not always how difficult it is to move around.

On the way home from the airport, Emma has long forgotten her worries and is really thrilled that Leila is finally there. She's staying for the whole week, because her parents are traveling and her school is on fall break. Emma is a little sad she'll have to go to school all week, but unfortunately school calendars don't always match up.

That evening they enjoy catching up. Leila is two years older than Emma and has just started attending Dutch secondary school this year. Emma listens patiently to all of Leila's stories about her new school and all the boys she likes. She likes a lot of boys. At first Leila takes little interest in Emma's new life, but Emma doesn't mind too much. She takes comfort in the familiarity of Leila's stories.

Finally, after about an hour, Leila begins to ask Emma a bit about her new school. Emma begins to explain how everyone is from a different place.

"Are there any cute boys in your new class?" Leila asks.

Emma hesitates and feels her face going red like a tomato.

"Oh, come on, 'fess up!" Leila says.

"Well, there is this one really nice Swedish boy called Elias," Emma says, unsure of how to talk about boys.

"And are you good friends, already?" Leila asks.

"Not really, but I'm just starting to get to know people," Emma reminds her.

"You know what you should do?" Leila asks, always ready with a solution before Emma even understands the problem, "You should have a party for your birthday next month and invite him as well!"

Before falling asleep, Emma thinks about Leila's comment. *Not such a bad idea, maybe it will help me get to know some people a little better.* Emma was eager to make some closer friends.

The next afternoon, Mom picks Emma up from school on her own.

"Where is Leila?" Emma asks.

"Oh, she wanted to finish a book she was reading, so I left her at home. She's very excited for you to come back though. I think she was a little bored without you today."

As soon as they arrive home, Mom puts the kettle on and prepares tea. She also puts out the *speculaas;* cookies that Leila brought with her. As the three of them sit around the kitchen table, Emma tells a little about her day.

"What about you, Leila?" she asks, "What have you been up to?"

"Oh, not much, but I was wondering," Leila asks, "why you're being driven to school? Can't you bike like everyone else?"

Mom takes a moment to sip her Earl Grey tea, then looks at Leila lovingly. "Everyone else here is being driven to school as well, sweetie. It's not like the Netherlands," she says.

"That's ridiculous. Just because Emma goes to a fancy international school doesn't mean she doesn't know how to bike anymore, right?" Leila asks in a disdainful yet truly puzzled tone.

Emma looks at Mom desperately and isn't sure how to reply.

"Right," Mom answers, "you're making a good point, and Emma certainly still knows how to bike. You know what though, Leila, Emma needs to go do some homework and as we only have one bike, would you be a sweetheart and go get me a newspaper from the little shop? It's not far from here, a ten-minute bike ride to town and back. You can handle that, right?"

"Well, of course, *tante,* no problem," Leila says confidently as she takes the money Mom is holding out to her. "Just tell me where to go."

Emma hears Mom explaining the route to Leila as she heads up to her room to start working on her homework. She is smiling to herself, as she completely understands what Mom is up to.

From the upstairs balcony, Emma watches Leila whizzing down the street with her legs sticking out on both sides of the bike as she flies down the hill.

About thirty minutes later, she hears Leila put the bike back in the garage. Mom walks in to help her. Emma hears Mom ask Leila if she would like a glass of water. When Emma walks into the kitchen she sees a very sweaty and red-faced Leila. She obviously doesn't need to ask her if now she understands why Emma doesn't bike to school.

"Hmmph," Leila mutters, out of breath. After gulping down a glass of water, Leila turns to her aunt and cousin.

"All right. Point made."

Emma and Mom look at Leila and suddenly burst out laughing. Leila looks at them slightly annoyed, but cannot help but join in.

"WHY DO YOU CALL HIM B?" B HEARS CAROLYN ASK EMMA.
"I mean he's hardly a bee, right?" Carolyn is holding B,
flipping him around and curiously inspecting him.

The first week or two at her new school had been
very exciting. The kids who greeted Emma a few
months ago were eager to have her join their group.
She also made some friends in her ESL class; English as
a Second Language. Principal Evans had encouraged
her to join the ESL class three times a week, just for
the first semester, to help her improve a little faster.
She didn't really mind. After all, Elias was also in the
small class.

Emma felt very welcome, but the initial euphoria
of all the new places, people and things wore off.

Emma started to long for that familiar feeling she had found in Stolwijk. It goes without saying that she turned to B quite often. It had helped that Leila had been to visit, but her presence had made Emma almost want to go back to the Netherlands even more.

However, over the last couple of weeks, things have taken a turn for the better. Late night chats with B are being replaced by phone calls to her new friends. Carolyn is one of them and B isn't too sure if he likes her. Perhaps now that she's visiting, he can get to know her a little better.

Emma explains how B got his nickname. B has always liked his name. When Emma is looking for B, Daan often replies with the Shakespeare quote, 'To be, or not to be, that is the question'.

Bee, the English definition of his name that Carolyn suggested, had never crossed his mind. He always prefers to think of himself as B as in 'to be'. It doesn't matter where he's from or where he's going, all that matters is to be. Whenever Emma feels conflicted about who she is and where she belongs, he feels like screaming out: "Just be yourself, that's all you need to be!"

Names are peculiar. They are part of who we are, influence our identity and may take on special meanings. If our own name is misunderstood or mispronounced by others, all that matters is how meaningful it is to us. *Bee, pfff,* B thinks to himself, *Buzz off! I am* B. *And proud of it!*

"So, do you still sleep with your B?" B hears Carolyn ask with slight amazement. *Was she mocking Emma? Or him?* B wonders.

B almost decides Emma's made an unfortunate choice of companion, when he hears Carolyn admit, "I still sleep with my rabbit, Bunny."

"You do?" Emma asks, relieved she's not the only one.

"Oh sure, since the day I was born. My sisters always make fun of me, but I don't care. He's just way too cuddly to part with."

B instantly likes Carolyn and her rabbit. Even he judges too quickly sometimes.

"Yeah, B is like that. I can't really sleep well without him. I use him as a pillow and when he's not there, it doesn't seem right," B hears Emma say.

"Same here! Sometimes I get a little embarrassed about it though. So whenever I have a sleepover, I leave him at home." Carolyn puts B back down on Emma's bed. "Speaking of sleepovers! Have you decided if you're going to have one for your birthday?" Carolyn asks.

Emma will be turning eleven this November. *She is growing up much too fast!* B thinks. Just like Carolyn, Emma might soon decide she can't be seen with her teddy bear any more. *Or worse, what if she won't need me at all?* he wonders.

"My parents said I could invite ten people. So I'm thinking of asking all of our usual crew, and Emad and Sasha from my ESL class," Emma begins to explain. "I don't think the boys would be allowed to stay for a sleepover, but I'm sure my parents would let all the girls stay."

"That sounds like fun! And what do you want to do for the party?" Carolyn asks.

"Well, in Holland, we usually have everybody over for the afternoon. There are games or a treasure hunt, and then we eat cake," Emma explains. "Perhaps we can watch a movie in the evening, what do you think?"

"Wait a minute, Holland? I thought you said you were from the Netherlands?" Carolyn asks, looking confused.

"I guess we sometimes say Holland, because it's shorter and easier to say, but Holland is actually only a small part of the Netherlands."

B continues to listen to the party plans, but slowly tunes out. He is happy Emma's making new friends. He hopes she'll now begin to realize home might physically change, but that she will always feel at home wherever she finds friends. Together with her family and new friends, memories are formed at each new place and little roots are grown along with them.

Settling In

"All right, everyone, get ready to sing!" Mom yells from the kitchen. Dad switches the lights off in the dining room.

"Which languages will you chose, Emma?" Drew asks. Whenever there is a birthday at school, their teacher, Mr Harper, always allows the class to sing 'Happy Birthday' in three languages. The tradition is carried on to parties as well.

"Ehmmmm, Japanese, Polish ..." Emma says, "and, ehmmm, Swedish." She tries not to look at Elias, fearing her crush is becoming obvious.

As they all try to sing along to the foreign versions of the birthday song, Mom walks in with her cake. Mom doesn't like to bake, but every year she puts a big effort into Emma's cake. For ideas, the two of them went through what seemed like hundreds of pictures of cakes on Pinterest. Finally, they came upon one of an artist's palette, very much like the one Emma loves to use. Mom added 11 different colors of icing onto the first layer of chocolate frosting. In each color she had stuck a candle that looked like a small paintbrush. The sides were covered with M&M's and a small cup filled with forks was placed in the hole you would use to hold the palette. Everyone looks at it in admiration and Emma is beaming.

"Your cake is so cool!" Emad, Emma's new friend from Pakistan, exclaims as Mom puts it down on the table.

"Oh, I love M&M's!" Carolyn adds. Mom looks proud.

"All right, Emma. Make a wish!" Keiko says.

Emma smiles and looks at the eleven burning candles. She closes her eyes tight and makes her wish.

"What is it? What is it?" Sasha, an outgoing girl who moved to Luxembourg from Russia only a few weeks ago, inquires nosily with a cheeky grin.

"I can't tell you that!" Emma feels her cheeks burn a little, but knows never to tell your wishes.

Mom starts cutting the cake and they all sit around the big round table. At the center of the table a box, wrapped in colorful paper and ribbons, is waiting for Emma.

Karen takes the lead. "We decided to get you a

present together instead of a few little things. We really hope you'll like it," she says.

"Come on, open it!" Geoff encourages Emma.

Carefully Emma unwraps the gift. It's a globe of the Earth, but it doesn't look like the usual globes at school. She takes it out of the box and takes a good look it.

"It changes colors when you press the button!" Lynda excitedly says, pointing out a little black button on the North Pole.

"And look, in its base there's a little drawer!" Elias says. He reaches over and pulls the drawer out for her. Inside are small map tacks. "Here you go," he says, handing her a red tack, "you can mark every place you travel to by putting a pin into the globe!" he says.

"Or move to," Karen adds.

"Dad, can you switch the lights off again, please?" Emma enthusiastically asks.

In the dark room they all watch the globe turn blue, then green, violet, and about six other colors.

"It reminds me of a chameleon!" Aneta whispers.

Perfect! Emma thinks. Only the other day, she started writing in her journal that she sometimes felt like a chameleon, fitting into almost every group of people she ever met, blending in everywhere and anywhere. Problem is, she can't help but wonder which of the colors are truly hers. She needs to explore the parts of her that always seem to stay the same no matter where she goes on this big planet.

"It makes me want to travel lots!" Drew says, staring at the globe in awe.

"When I grow up, I want to travel around the world with a backpack after high school. My oldest sister is doing that right now," Carolyn says.

"Where is she now?" Keiko asks.

"Africa." Carolyn turns the globe and puts her index finger on the big continent. "My sister says that the list of places where she wants to travel has only grown since she started backpacking. She thought she would cross places off, but finds she is always adding news ones, so the list never gets shorter."

"Sounds nice," Elias jumps in, "but sometimes I feel like our family has traveled so much already, I wish we could stay in one place for a while. We've moved so often I don't really feel like we have roots anywhere. It's the traveling and moving around that has become a home of sorts," Elias looks at Karen, who nods in agreement.

"I know exactly what you mean, Elias," Emma says quietly, looking around the table. "But I can't imagine always living in one place either. If I had, I would have never met you guys," she adds.

"Good thing you moved here then!" Emad says and the others all concur, smiling. For a moment Emma's and Elias' eyes meet. It almost seems as if he is feeling a little shy too.

"Thank you so much for this gift! I absolutely love

it!" Emma takes out a pin from the drawer and sticks it into the little tiny country of Luxembourg.

"Okay, I think everyone has a slice of cake and a drink in front of them. Dig in!" Dad says. "Let me turn the lights back on."

"All right! Let's eat!" Emma says, eagerly sticking her fork into her big piece of chocolate cake.

As Emma and her new friends sit around eating the entire palette, she thinks back to the 'Where are you from?' conversation on the day she first visited the school. She realizes she'll never be able to simply say, 'I'm from the Netherlands'. Of course, she is originally Dutch, but she lives in Luxembourg, and somehow she also still feels at home in Switzerland. She fits in everywhere and belongs nowhere. *I guess all of us at this table are from somewhere in between here and everywhere,* Emma thinks. And knowing that every single person around the table understands what she means makes her feel very much at home.

B IS WATCHING EMMA CRAMMING HER CLOTHES INTO a bag. It's almost Christmas and Emma's winter break started yesterday. Mom and Dad are busy packing up the car, making sure it's all set so they can leave early tomorrow morning.

"Hmmm, one pair of jeans or two?"

B listens to Emma ask herself as she pulls clothes out of her closet. Her ski gear is already in a bag Mom packed, but Emma's supposed to pack the rest of the things she wants to take.

B cannot wait to go back to Gryon again. He loves watching the familiar mountains through all the seasons, but winter is definitely his favorite. Everything looks so peaceful in white. He also loves returning to the same place each year. Both Emma and he have built memories in that little Swiss town since she was four years old. It has really become the one home they always come back to.

B watches Emma arrange all the clothes before stuffing them in the bag Mom gave her. It fills up awfully quickly.

"Hmmm," Emma says to herself, "maybe if I sit on it?"

"What are you doing?" Mom asks, walking in as Emma plops on top of her bag on her knees.

"The bag's not big enough!" Emma complains.

"Or, maybe," Mom asks, "you tried to pack too much?" Mom opens the bag and sorts through Emma's clothes. "Emma, it's a vacation! Not a move." Mom laughs and removes a couple of sweaters and a few shirts. She zips the bag up without a problem. "Here you go. Can I take it down to the car now?"

"Yes, thanks, Mom," Emma says. "I'll pack my books and all the things for the ride in my backpack."

"Okay. Don't forget to put your Moving Booklet in your bag. Remember, Charlotte asked about it?" Mom reminds Emma.

Charlotte and her parents are going to be staying at their ski hut this Christmas, so Emma and her parents have rented a small apartment close by. *She must be so excited to see Charlotte,* B thinks.

"Oh, that's right! I can't wait to tell her that Mr Harper emailed *Juf* Anja to ask if he could make a Moving Booklet for Aneta when she told him she's moving back to Poland," Emma responds.

B has heard quite a bit about Mr Harper these days. He's a lot stricter than *Juf* Anja, but he can also be really funny.

"Maybe you girls can send *Juf* Anja a postcard from the mountain," Mom suggests as she walks out of the door. "I bet she'd love that."

"Right. But before I do anything else, I'm going to finish what I started before packing!" Emma says, looking at B as if he has to hold her to that decision.

Even if he could, he doesn't need to. Emma is already sitting on her bed and B is moved to his usual spot, between Emma's head and the wall. Her Moving Booklet is turned to the very last page. The title reads: 'Half the new school year is done! How I feel now'. When Emma is done writing, she reads it aloud to B.

"Stolwijk has now become a place of memories, and our new house here in Steinsel is slowly starting to feel more like home. I'm not going to get too attached to it though, because I know I'll have to say goodbye to these walls at some point. Dad and I planted a chestnut tree in the garden and I love watching it grow. I guess right now I am home here, but when we arrive in Gryon I will be home there too. Home is not necessarily one place. It's all the places that are a part of me. Home is all of my experiences combined. Home is in all the languages I speak. Home is all the people I hold so close in my heart. Home is always with me."

B watches Emma draw a big 'T' below the paragraph she just wrote. He smiles to himself, watching the pros side outnumber the cons side this time.

Pros	Cons
Had an amazing going away party!	Sad to leave
Great new friends from all over!	Saying goodbye to friends
Love my new school	Saying goodbye to school
Huge room with pink carpet	Saying goodbye to house
Chestnut tree outside my window	Leaving owls
On the school's swimming team	No more tennis and swimming
English almost fluent, no more ESL after winter break!	
Great 11th birthday party	
Really nice neighborhood kids	
Someone from Juf Anja's new class wants to become pen pals	
Mimi will come visit in February	
I think I'm learning to figure out where I belong	

Early the next morning, B hears Mom yelling, "Emma, we're leaving! Are you ready?" from the bottom of the stairs.

"Coming!"

B watches Emma quickly stuff her Moving Booklet and a few books in her backpack. Then he hears her hurry down the stairs.

Whoa! Wait a minute! he thinks to himself. *Is this it? Is this the moment where she forgets to take me on a trip?* Then he hears Emma's footsteps running back up the stairs.

"What did you forget?" Mom yells after her.

"Nothing! Will be right down!"

Nothing? Nonsense! B thinks.

"The most important thing!" Emma whispers to B, grabbing him from the bed. She gives him a tight hug and runs back downstairs, out of the door and straight into the car. She tosses B next to Gypsy, who is already sprawled out on the back seat and seems reluctant to share.

"Everybody ready for a vacation in the mountains?" Dad asks from behind the wheel.

"Yes!" Mom and Emma say in unison. Gypsy lazily moves his big hairy head on top of B's. *Why does everyone do this to me?* B thinks, but inside he feels as excited about this trip as the rest of the family. In case anyone wonders, he says to himself, *to me, home is everything I ever hoped for.*

The End

Glossary of Dutch Words

bakkie koffie – cup of coffee

gezellig – difficult to translate but its nearest translation is 'cozy' or something with a nice atmosphere

Goudse kaas – a type of Dutch cheese

Juf – informal title for a female teacher

maatje – grandmother

oom – uncle

paatje – grandfather

speculaas – a type of Dutch cookie

Sinterklaas – (Feast of St Nicholas) an annual Dutch celebration on December 5th when children receive gifts

tante – aunt

tot morgen – see you tomorrow

Discussion Questions

Use the discussion questions below to get more out of the experience of reading *B at Home* by Valérie Besanceney:

1. Emma says to B "I just want to be home" (p.9). What does B think she means? What do you think this means?

2. Emma's parents say they understand it will be difficult for Emma to "leave this life behind" (p.15). Do you think her parents really understand? Why would it be difficult for her parents to fully understand Emma's concerns? What can they do to find out what they are?

3. Once Emma has written up her 'pros and cons list' she comes to the conclusion that it won't really convince her parents (p.19). Why not?

4. B speaks about the 'serendipity of life' (p.37). What do you think this means?

5. B likes to think that it's "... each of our little idiosyncrasies that makes us unique" (p.25). Through the context of this sentence, can you explain what the word 'idiosyncrasy' means? Can you think of any idiosyncrasies you or any of your friends have that make you special?

6. B contemplates the word friendship: "Friendships were like ships moving from shore to shore, never staying anchored in one port for a very long time." (p.94). When you move, do you think friendships can last? What can you do to make sure they do?

7. Emma's mother had a friend make a 'memory quilt' for Emma. She also encourages Emma to create the collage on her desk. Why do you think keepsakes are important when you move?

8. Emma's parents try to involve Emma in making certain decisions, like which school to go to and what house they'll live in. How else could parents empower their children when moving?

9. Saying goodbye properly is such an important part of a transition. Why do you think it is?

10. Emma's friends organize a goodbye party for her and give her a pillow that is signed by all her classmates. If you moved, how do you think you would like to say your goodbyes?

11. If Emma were your friend, what would you do to help her through her "roller coaster of feelings" (p.56)?

12. Learning a new language is always a challenge. Have you ever felt 'lost in translation' like Emma did on her first day of school in Zurich?

13. There are many advantages to becoming a polyglot (someone who knows different languages) at an early age. Can you think of some?

14. Are there any words like *gezellig* in your language that are not easily translated?

15. Emma uses several similes to describe how she feels about moving and home. For example, "Like the waves, like the beads in the kaleidoscope." (p.21). Can you think of your own similes to describe what a move or home feels like to you?

16. Emma and her friends talk about how certain smells bring back memories. What are some smells that bring back strong memories for you?

17. If you could help *Juf* Anja make a Moving Booklet what would you include?

18. In her Introduction, Valérie Besanceney says that only a handful of teachers showed empathy (p.xx). What can teachers and administrators in schools do better to help students when they move?

19. When Emma moves to Luxembourg she hosts a birthday party to get to know people better. What are some other things you could do to get to know people better?

20. When talking about planting trees, Emma's father says, "it will also remind you of how you have grown ..." (p.81). What does he mean? How has Emma grown during this move?

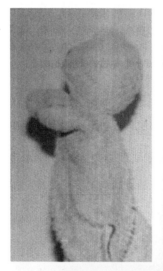

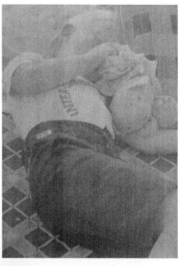

Photos (clockwise from top left):

B when Valérie was born

B and Valérie (when she was a little younger than Emma)

B today

About the Author

Originally Dutch, Valérie Besanceney grew up changing schools and countries five times as a child. These days, Valérie loves teaching Year 3 at an international school. Whenever any of her students move away, she makes them a Moving Booklet.

B still hangs out on the quilt on her bed. At one point, he was barely hanging together by a few threads, so Mom sewed him onto another bear to save what was left of him.

Valérie is a quintessential third culture kid (TCK) turned adult. She has made a home, together with her American husband and their two daughters, in Switzerland. If you also feel like home is somewhere in between here and everywhere, or if you would like to learn more about TCKs, please visit her at www.valeriebesanceney.com.

Also by Summertime Publishing

A Global Nomad's Journey From Hurt To Healing

Letters

NEVER SENT

RUTH E. VAN REKEN

MORE THAN 32,000 COPIES SOLD

The Mission of Detective Mike
Moving Abroad

Lightning Source UK Ltd.
Milton Keynes UK
UKOW02f1012030616

275526UK00003B/15/P